Death

Date

To Sara,
What would you do if you knew
your Death Date?

Ashe Taylor

Ashe Taylor

Table Of Contents

Prologue

History exists in the minds and stories of those who lived it. We pass on our experiences from generation to generation, hoping to teach the lessons that we learned along the way. Children are taught about the ordeals and accomplishments their ancestors went through. In schools, teachers instruct their students using textbooks created by those who lived through the stories found within the pages. There are many anecdotes that can be found in these books, but the whole truth won't be in there. From what I have heard over the years, no one ever tells the whole truth, especially when it comes to the history of our world.

It wasn't so long ago that society functioned in a very different way from how it is now. The schoolbooks only go so far back in time, making sure not to give away too much information to young, impressionable minds. If you want to really know how we got to where we are now, well, you have to travel the Underground. I hadn't planned to venture down that path, but my desire to find out more than what I was given led me there. It would turn out to be quite the wild ride, and one that would change the course of my life.

It was on that trip that I discovered who I really was, and what I was destined to do. The experiences I underwent while on my journey led me to the life I lead now. It is my story, but I am only one character in it. I doubt my narrative will ever come to light, as the truth would be too much for many to bear. There is only one question that is still left unanswered. Given the chance, would I do it all again?

Part One

Background

Chapter One

Adelaine Kingston

"Hey Del, do you remember anything about when you got your chip put in?" my little sister Davina asked me, poking her head out of her bedroom door.

"Not really, why?" I answered as I fumbled around in my pocket, trying to find the hair tie I had stuck in there earlier. I had a serious case of bed head, and my thick, unruly curls were attacking my cheeks.

"I'm supposed to do a report for school, and my teacher loves it when someone uses a primary source. High school teachers want only the best, I guess. I thought maybe I could interview you, but if you don't remember, then don't worry about it."

"Yeah, sorry. I was only about three when I got it, and I don't remember much from that time at all." I stretched onto my toes while reaching up to the second shelf. All of the workouts I had been doing kept my body goals in check, but they didn't provide me with any extra height. Short girl syndrome is a very real

4

thing. Grabbing my mug, I walked over to the coffee machine and started it up.

"No worries. Guess I'll just have to do my research elsewhere." She disappeared again, closing her door behind her. The smell of warm hazelnut filled the air as the first drops fell into my cup.

I felt badly that I couldn't help her. Most kids her age would probably just speak with their parents, but Davina wasn't that lucky. Our dad died just a few hours after she was born, and mom never remarried. She always refused to talk about it, though. We learned not to mention it anymore after she had an absolute screaming fit at us the last time we brought it up. That was about five years ago.

Life wasn't easy with my mom, but I know that she always tried to do her best by us. Raising two children as a single mom was emotionally straining. No matter how hard she tried, she always had to make sure there was a contingency plan in place for us in case they activated her chip before we were old enough to be on our own. She could never let her guard down, and she wasn't ever really able to enjoy life since she was so scared.

There were nine years between Davina and me. While not unwanted, my sister certainly wasn't planned. My mom was only twenty-three when she gave birth to me, the same age I am now. It feels weird to imagine myself as a mom right now. My mother had just graduated from college the year before and received her degree in veterinary medicine. She loved all animals, and looked forward to becoming a veterinarian in the near future. She met my dad while she was in her junior year of college, and they fell in love very quickly. They became engaged after only dating a few months, and got married within a year. The plan was to wait to have children until after my mother had graduated from veterinary school, so she could work and raise a family at the same time. She had just started school when she found out she was pregnant with me. She was surprised, but decided that she would finish school while raising a family at the same time.

During her pregnancy, my mother continued her studies. Once I was born, she realized how hard it would be for her to finish. She was able to find care for me while she was in class, but never got a moment to herself to do her schoolwork with a baby around. When I wasn't screaming for something, I would sleep peacefully, but only in her arms. If she dared to try to put me in my crib, I was instantly awake and screaming again. Once I learned to crawl, the whole game changed as my little hands got into everything. Being a curious little one, I was always on the go, trying to discover new things. When my mother realized I was getting ready to walk and she couldn't keep up with both her assignments and me she made the tough decision to quit school. She intended to go back at some point, but it just never happened. By the time I had turned about four years old, my dad was making enough money as a computer programmer that she was able to stay home comfortably. The desire to be a veterinarian was still there, but the drive was gone.

My childhood with my parents wasn't anything out of the ordinary; I would describe

7

my life as pretty typical. When I started school at the age of five, they gave me some tests and told my parents that I was what they called *gifted*. Apparently, my scores were really high, and they wanted to advance me several grades. My parents were worried that I wouldn't fit in with the older kids, so they agreed to just putting me one year ahead of where I was supposed to be according to the school calendar. I continued to get high grades, and the work was way too easy for me. At the end of third grade, they advanced me once again, putting me in fifth grade when I was only eight years old.

It was hard to be so much younger than my classmates were, so I didn't end up having very many friends. While the other kids were having playdates and hanging out, I could usually be found tucked away in my room with a good book, or playing whatever video game I could get my hands on. Since I was an only child the first nine years of my life, most of the fun I had was on my own. My dad liked video games too, so he would join me when he could for a battle royale. My parents did a good job making sure my life at home wasn't any different from other kids.

I remember when mom told me that she was pregnant. I had gotten so used to being the only child; I have to admit that I was a little bit angry that I would have to share my parents with someone else. Especially since I didn't really have friends, they were my playing companions. At the same time, it was exciting to think that I would have a little sister or brother to play with. After all of these years, I finally wouldn't feel so alone. The day my mother went into labor, my dad went into major freak out mode. You would think that Davina was his first child the way he was acting. Pacing back and forth so quickly, I thought he was going to wear out a path in the floor. I guess it all seemed new again to him since it had been so long from when I first arrived.

We got to the hospital, and they got mom all set up in her room. There were several wires attached to her, monitoring both my mom and my future sibling's heartbeats. Since I was too young to be in there during delivery, one of her friends came and stayed with me in the waiting area so dad could go in. I had my gaming system, along with a bag full of books and games to switch out. Those, along with enough money to keep buying treats and drinks, kept me busy while we waited. I didn't pay much attention to my mom's friend. She seemed nice, allowing me to eat several candy bars and drink soda. The bubbles tickled my nose, but the flavor made the suffering worth it. Time seemed to fly by while my brain focused on other things, and before I knew it, dad had come out to get us.

He brought me in alone first, and I will never forget how proud he looked as he introduced me to Davina, my new little sister. He told me how it would be up to me as the big sister to teach her all the ways of the world. How she would look up to me, so I had to set a good example for her. To me, she was just this beautiful little bundle. Her terra-cotta skin shone in the light, as if the universe had imbued her body with flames from inside. Her deep, dark eyes were full and bright, and she had a head full of tiny curls. She was the perfect blend of features from our parents, a combination of our mother's darker features and our father's lighter ones. I saw her as a smaller version of myself, similar in looks, but different enough to be distinct. Any negative feelings I might have had about getting a sibling instantly melted away when my eyes first met hers.

Right away, we took pictures of Davina and the entire family. Next, we made phone calls to friends and family to announce the newest arrival. My mother's friend eventually joined us in the room, staying for a short while before making her exit as I could now stay with my family. Everyone wanted to come up and visit, but my mother needed to rest a bit first. After a couple of hours of sleep, she said she was ready to have guests. I sat on the small bench in the room that folded out into a bed. It wasn't very soft, and I wondered if dad would be uncomfortable sleeping on it that night. My grandparents were going to be arriving later that evening. The plan was for them to stay at the house with me while my dad stayed at the hospital with mom and Davina.

My dad had just returned from getting some food from the cafeteria for us when suddenly he collapsed to the floor. The trays he was holding went flying through the air, and I watched as my burger and French fries landed on the tiles next to him. My mother screamed, and I ran to his side, calling out for him. One of the nurses must have heard the commotion, as they came running into the room. They stopped when they saw my father on the ground, and looked at my mother. Kneeling down beside me, they checked for a pulse, but couldn't find one.

"Oh no, I am so sorry" was all they said, touching their hand on my mother's arm for a brief moment, and then leaving the room. They didn't do anything to help him, almost as if they knew this was going to happen. My mother got out of bed and joined me at his side. She was running her fingers through my dad's hair, and she just kept saying the same things repeatedly.

"No, this can't be happening! Not today! This can't be right! "

I didn't know much about death at only nine years old, but I knew that my dad was gone. Several people entered the room, one rolling in a gurney, and another carrying a white sheet with a small tag laying on top of it. One of the nurses escorted me out and into the hallway. He sat me down and asked if I had anyone else there besides my parents. When I told him that my grandparents were on their way, he told me to sit tight, and someone would come and stay with me. He walked a few steps away, keeping one eye on me the whole time, and picked up a phone. I couldn't hear what he was saying, but his face showed both sadness and concern. A minute later, the people that were in the room with my mom had started to walk out, taking with them the gurney that had my dad's covered body on it. He was gone, and they were rolling his lifeless form away.

Someone who they told me was a social worker had come to sit with me around the same time, and she asked if I understood what was going on. I explained to her that I knew that my dad had died, and that some people had taken his body away. At the time, I didn't really know too much about how the chips worked, but I would find out soon after that. The social worker spoke with one of the nurses that had been in with my mom. She asked if I was ready to go back in the room, and I said yes. All I wanted at that point was to be back with my mother. When I went in, she seemed much calmer than I had expected her to be. They told me that they gave her some medicine to help her relax, and that she would probably be falling asleep soon so she could get some more rest. The social worker said she would stay in the room with me so my mom could sleep.

"Where is Davina?" I questioned of the woman who seemed glued to my side.

"She's safe in the nursery, where she's been all of this time."

"Can I see her?"

"I can take you there right now if you'd like to go."

Of course, I said yes, and the social worker took my hand as we approached the elevator. She stopped at the nurse's station and let someone know where we would be so my mom wouldn't worry.

When we arrived at the nursery, I spent a while just looking at her through the window, trying to find some peace while my entire body was freaking out. Here was this new life, and according to what some of my dad's last words were to me, I was responsible for her. I felt the weight of the world on my nine-year-old frame, and I thought I was going to crumble.

After some time had passed, the social worker brought me to an area where they had some games and a television set up for kids. She hung out with me until my grandparents arrived, then left the room once they had been brought up to speed. My grandma held me in her arms and wept openly. My grandpa gave me a big hug, and then he left to go and see my mom. So much had already happened that day, and I was ready to go home. I didn't want to leave my mother and sister, though. I begged to be able to stay just the one night, but I was told that the hospital didn't allow it. My grandma brought me to my mother's room, where I snuggled up beside her as she held

Davina. I stayed in that spot for as long as they let me, and then gave them both hugs and kisses before leaving with my grandpa. My grandma was going to spend the night at the hospital with mom, as they allowed the adults to stay, and they didn't want my mom to be all alone.

I remember it being hard to sleep at home, and I spent most of the late night hours crying next to my grandpa. We laid together on the guest bed that was set up in the nursery. He held me as my eyes emptied themselves of the pain they held inside. Surrounding us were bright pictures of owls, the theme of my sister's new room. They all looked so happy, perched on the branches of painted on trees against a beautiful blue background. It was so hard to fully enjoy the birth of my sister when my father had just died. I had so many questions, but was too worried that I would upset someone if I asked any of them. As I thought about all of the wonderful memories I had with my dad, I realized that Davina would never get any of those for herself. She would grow up never knowing the love of the man who made up half of who she was. I tried hard not to focus on that, as it just made things even worse.

The next morning, my grandpa let me ride with him back to the hospital to go and pick mom and Davina up. Since dad's car was still parked in the hospital lot, I rode back to the house in his car with grandpa, and grandma took my mom and sister to the house. The car still smelled like my dad, and I inhaled deeply as I settled into my seat. Would this be the last time I would get to smell him? What else would suddenly disappear? It was great having everyone home together, but with dad gone, it felt incomplete. Davina spent most of the day being held in someone's arms, and I focused on the new video game that my grandparents bought me as a big sister gift. It wasn't that I didn't want to spend time with the family. It's just that they were doing a lot of planning for the future and talking about things like finances. There was no need for me to be around for those conversations, and I'm sure they didn't mind me leaving them alone to discuss the adult stuff.

They all agreed that grandma and grandpa would stay a bit longer than they had originally planned so they could help get things organized. Their being there also helped to keep mom a little saner during what was probably the hardest part of her life. The simplest tasks like laundry became weights tied to her feet, dragging her down. I tried to help out by doing things such as cleaning up without being asked to, and pitching in with the cooking. I was in school during most of the day, though, so my assistance was limited.

The day that my grandparents left, there was a shift in the dynamics in our home. Mom was still the parent, but I felt like I had taken on the role of being her caregiver. She always seemed to carry around a certain sadness, even when she was smiling and laughing. There was a part of her personality that she was trying to push away, but it kept creeping back up. I wanted to be there for her and for Davina, but I wasn't sure exactly how to do that. Mom seemed more withdrawn, and there were times when I was worried she wasn't able to take care of Davina properly. I quickly learned how to feed and change my sister, at times acting more like her mother than her sibling.

The first month as a new family of three, many people came around to check on us. After receiving my father's ashes, we held a small memorial service for our loved ones to attend so they could say their goodbyes. People continued to come around following that for the next few weeks, bringing meals and offering to help clean up the house. Since mom had fallen into a mild depression, the upkeep of the house was left mostly to me. It didn't take long, though, before the number of visitors started dwindling down. They moved on with their lives, and we were expected to do the same.

Eventually we all fell into a routine and as the months and years moved on, mom adjusted to being a single mom of two. The money that was left behind when dad died helped us out for the first couple of years, but then it became obvious that we wouldn't make it unless mom started working again. Having never lost her love of working with animals, she was able to find a job as a veterinary assistant at a local animal hospital. As much as it pained her to do it, she placed Davina in a day care that the overseers subsidized, and she only worked while I was in school. When Davina was old enough to start school, she increased her hours a bit, and I would take care of the two of us when we got home each day for a few hours. Mom made sure she was always home in time to make dinner, and we treasured our time together as a family each night. We were no longer just surviving, we were actually thriving.

***

Over the years, mom dated a few men here and there, but never settled down with anyone. I don't think anyone could ever match up to the wonderful man my dad was. My mother had high standards, and no one else could compare to the gold star she fell in love with so many years ago. I tried to get her to go out more and meet people, but the struggle wasn't worth the fight. At least she had her girls' nights to help her recognize all parts of her identity.

When I was fifteen, I entered my senior year of high school. There were several pamphlets and brochures laid out across the table for me to start planning on which college I wanted to attend. I didn't feel ready, but it wasn't an option that I was given. My mother expected, nay, demanded that I go to a university and get my degree. She constantly reminded me how smart I was, and that I was not about to waste the amazing brain that I was given. While things had settled down in our home, I was worried that if I suddenly up and left, my mom wouldn't know what to do with Davina on her own. She would have to cut back on her hours, and with the cost of tuition, I didn't know how she would be able to afford everything.

I applied for, and fortunately received, several scholarships. Due to being a young graduate, many schools were eager to have me attend. Most of them were happy to offer full rides once they read my application essay that detailed all that my family had been through. My mother insisted that I apply to schools that weren't close by so that I could get the full experience of being a college student. I would only be sixteen when I graduated, and I didn't feel quite ready for adult status yet. Still, I did as she said, and ended up choosing a university that required a plane flight to get home. All of those years of playing video games led me to choose computer science as my major. I was curious to learn the behind the scenes details, and hoped to one day maybe even create my own game. The list of courses I would be taking really piqued my interest, and made me think that my mother might actually have been right in pushing me to go. It was almost like learning an entirely new language, something that intrigued me.

Even with all of the excitement I felt about starting this new path in my life, it didn't take long for me to realize that college was not the right path for me. Being so much younger than everyone else really took its toll on the entire experience. The professors did not take me seriously, my classmates didn't want anything to do with me, and I couldn't really go anywhere since I wasn't driving yet. I tried really hard to make it work, but it was a daily struggle. I was sharing a room with an eighteen-year-old girl who looked at me as more of an annoying little sister than a peer. She wanted to stay up late and party, and I just wanted to get my work done (not that anyone wanted me at their parties, either). After six months of what could be equated to as mild torture, I decided to drop out of school.

My mom was very disappointed in me, but I pointed out that there were several benefits to having me back home. I was able to take on a job while Davina was in school, and then be sure to be home when she got back. That allowed my mom to increase her hours to what they were previously. Between that and my paycheck, we had a nice amount of money coming in. I didn't like working, as the only place that would take me in so young was a nearby family restaurant. I came home each day smelling of foreign foods whose names I could not pronounce. After a quick shower, I would help Davina with any work she needed to have done for school. While college wasn't my forte, I did enjoy learning. Thankfully, there was a library within walking distance of my job, so I was able to go and check out books before and after work each week.

I was still interested in computer science, so I tended to check out books in that genre. Over time, the realization hit me that coding was what I really wanted to focus on. I read everything I could get my hands on, which wasn't too much. I was able to locate a few websites that I could practice on, but most things that taught you how to use computers in any way that could lead to learning too much information had been shut down years ago. The overseers were very cautious when it came to allowing the citizens to gain knowledge. I had heard whispers of something called the Underground several times, but didn't know too much about it. I started to understand that if I really wanted to do anything worthwhile in computers, I would have to not only figure out what the Underground was, I would have to become a part of it.

Chapter Two

The Underground

I didn't know if it was an actual place, a secret society, or something else even more sinister. I didn't even know if it truly existed or not. All I knew was that if you wanted to find out something that the overseers didn't want you to, it usually could be found through the Underground. I heard there were little coded messages in some books that mentioned it, and some websites might refer to it. However, almost no one gave any details. I searched through almost everything I could think of to gather more information on it, but I always came up empty handed.

Shortly after my eighteenth birthday, my current employer, Prothymos, hired me. They are a gaming company, and I worked for them as a computer game programmer. It wasn't a super glamorous position, but it paid well, and I gained a lot of experience on the job. Mostly what I did was go through codes that other people have created and look for bugs, or mistakes that they might have done. My coworkers nicknamed me The Exterminator since I was always catching their slip ups. I'm sure it was a very sweet term of endearment.

I had moved out of my mother's house within weeks of starting that job, having saved up some money from working at the restaurant bit by bit over the last two years. Packing up my room, I tried hard not to cry as I looked around. Old stuffed animals with missing eyes from being loved on too much. Scuffed paint from the constant changing of posters as my tastes changed. My life was here, a steady constant for so long. Now I was digging up my roots and starting fresh. It was a scary prospect. It felt weird to leave them again, especially leaving Davina behind. She was nine years old, the same age I was when my world turned upside down. I felt so grown up then, but when I looked in her eyes, all I saw was a little girl. It pained me to walk out the door and say goodbye, but I knew that I had to get on with my life. I wanted a future where I could be successful in doing something that I actually loved. I had spent the last nine years taking care of my family, and it was time for me to do something that I desired for myself.

***

My dream of creating my own video game from scratch never went away, so I continued to work on it during my down time from the daily grind. I would start by sketching out pictures that I would imagine being displayed on the screen. I wrote notes on storylines, characters, and how I would envision the game play. Most of what I jotted down ended up in the recycling bin, deleting files as soon as I decided they weren't right. I didn't want to keep any ideas I didn't deem to be one hundred percent worthy of going into my game. I wanted perfection, and anything less than that wasn't worth keeping around.

I was fortunate to work with some great people at Prothymos, and I would bounce ideas off them occasionally. I wanted to be certain that no one tried to take my designs, so I made sure that everything I mentioned was put down in writing somewhere first. One of the people I worked with, Franklin, was an exceptional soundboard. Even though he was about 10 years older than me, I never felt like he treated me as someone who was beneath him. More of a mentor, he would ask me questions to get me to think through the finer details that perhaps I hadn't thought of before.

"Hey Franklin, what do you think of the idea of a VR game where you wore a full body suit that allowed you to interact completely with your environment?" I asked him one day while on our lunch break.

"It sounds cool in theory. Virtual reality is really popular, so you have that on your side. What exactly do you mean by interact with your environment? What would you be doing?"

"I was thinking of it being something like where you could build your own home, raise your own food supplies, and just engage in daily living activities." My mind was racing with thoughts about all of the things that could be done in the game, just like in life.

"Okay, that would be interesting. Would you be able to do it all from the very beginning, or would you have to work up through stages?"

"I figured you would have to work your way up, learning skills as you go that would enhance your playing experience. You know, just like in real life, where you have to crawl, then walk, then run." Honestly, I had only begun thinking about it. I hadn't worked out the details just yet.

"Would you be interacting with any other players, or just NPCs?" This is why I liked talking with him, he always thought of the different ways to create an idea.

"I thought it would be really cool if you could actually interact with other people who were logged in at the same time. It would be like you're in the same place at the same time, even if you're hundreds of miles apart in reality." I had big plans for this one idea, but I knew it would require a lot of work. "I have so many possibilities running around my brain. I would love to be able to make it so the players could fully immerse themselves in the world. A cool thing might be if they could experience some history, too. You know, go through things as they were several generations ago." The wheels in my head were spinning, making me feel slightly light headed.

"Yeah, I'm not sure if that'd be possible, Del. That sort of information is hard to come by." I sensed that he knew something I did not, so I had to try to find a way to coax it out of him.

"I know, but I'm sure there is *some* way I could get a hold of it. The history of the world didn't just disappear after all. There has to be some place where it's stored, tucked away for only certain eyes to see." I was hoping that he might want to offer something up without me having to ask him outright.

"Just be careful, you never know who might be listening." He leaned in closer to me, and I could feel his breath as it grazed my ear. "Come see me at the end of your shift. I might be able to help you out. Don't mention this to anyone, or you might end up *under ground*."

This was it! I was finally going to get some information on the most exclusive secret out there! I nodded to show that I understood, and we went our separate ways to return to work. I spent the next few hours giddy as I thought about what kinds of things I would discover once I learned more about the Underground. Having so much information become suddenly available to me was exciting in and of itself, but knowing it was such a dark secret made it even more exhilarating.

After I clocked out, I went up to Franklin, who still had another hour left to his shift. He told me to meet him at Teva Park at nine o'clock that night, and he would explain more to me then. I trusted him completely, so I agreed. It was dark when I arrived, but there were enough lights around the place to feel safe. I saw Franklin there waiting for me as I walked through the main gate. We went over to the swing set and each grabbed one to sit down upon.

"Del, I wanted you to meet me out here because I'm going to share some information with you that you have to swear not to tell anyone else. You can't even let people know that you have knowledge of this, regardless of whether they say they know it too or not." He was looking at me very seriously, so I knew this was no joke.

"I swear I won't tell anyone. I appreciate you even offering to share with me, and I will hold that sacred."

"Okay," he took a deep breath in. "You were right when you said earlier that the history of the world didn't just disappear. There are people who work with the overseers that have basically tried to make it look like it did, though. You see, the world was a very different place not too long ago. The system of law and order was not at all as it is now. People had more freedoms, and they were allowed to express their feelings about the things they didn't agree with more openly. The world changed drastically in a short amount of time, and most of those changes weren't really improvements. There are still people alive today who are old enough to remember what the world was like before. Of course, they know better than to speak about such things, as the fear of what would happen to them if they did is greater than the desire to pass on their history. There is only one place where you can find out anything dealing with the past if you want the truth. That's the Underground."

"So how do I get there? Is it a building of some sort?" I was thrilled that he finally said its name, but I still didn't know the specifics of what he was talking about.

"It's not a place, per se. It is more like a network. You can't walk into a building and find it, and you certainly cannot ask anyone about it. You have to be invited, and someone has to be the one to add you to it. I'm your invitation, and I will get you set up with it."

"This is really weird, but thanks for helping me. How will I know what to do?"

"There is a special browser you'll use to access the sites. From there, you can find groups of people to speak with if you wish to. Just remember, everyone on there was invited, but you never know who you can trust."

This was getting a bit creepy. Franklin told me that he would come by my house the next day after work and show me how to get it all set up. He made me promise with consequence of extreme circumstances not to mention our conversation to anyone. I did as I was told and said goodbye to him, leaving the park to head home. The next twenty-four hours couldn't pass by fast enough.

***

The next night Franklin showed up, right on time. My dog, Trixie, started yapping at the door as soon as she heard him walking up. That little white ball of fluff was the best companion, even if she was too small to really be a guard dog. I was glad I made the choice to adopt her after moving out. Having something to come home to each night made the stress of my daily life shrink a little bit. Franklin informed me that I was not allowed to watch him as he worked on my computer. It was really a matter of the less that I knew, the safer I was kind of thing. Trying to keep myself busy, I got us each something to drink, and threw together a couple of little platters of snacks. When those were done, I laid on the floor with Trixie, giving her belly rubs (her favorite). It didn't take as long as I thought it would before he told me that he was all done. He gave me a brief tutorial on how to get started, and then told me that it was up to me regarding how much I wanted to learn, and how far I wanted to travel in the Underground. Now that he had set me up, he took no responsibility for my actions from that moment on. It all sounded pretty scary, but I was eager to get started. I offered to have Franklin hang out a bit, but he said that he needed to get home, so I thanked him again and walked him to the entryway. As I closed the door behind him, he turned around and simply said, "Be safe".

I don't think I slept at all that night, as I spiraled down the rabbit hole of the Underground. The only times I left my desk were to let Trixie outside, grab a snack, or use the bathroom. I knew that there was a lot of information out there, but I had no clue how much truly existed. Every site I went to led me to at least a dozen more. The following hours were spent staring at the screen until my eyes glazed over and filled with tears that tried unsuccessfully to moisten the dry deserts on my face. Just as I felt like I was starting to doze off, my alarm notified me that it was time to get ready for work. I was absolutely whipped, and had no idea how I was going to make it through the day. Somehow, I managed to drag my body into the shower and clean up. Trixie stared at me as I did my best to become presentable, showing me her disapproval of my actions from the night before. My hair was thrown into a low-slung ponytail, and my standard uniform of jeans and a work polo left me ready to face what laid before me. I grabbed a couple of protein bars and an energy drink and headed out the door.

Opening my work locker, I tossed in my bag and snatched my lanyard. It had the worst picture of me on it, but the company wouldn't let me take another one. Since I needed the ID to get into restricted parts of the building, it was something I had to display at all times. Lucky me. I looked around for Franklin before realizing that he was off that day. Good, one less thing to worry about today. My body was yearning for bed, and my mind desired to be back at my computer, taking a ride through the Underground. I just had to make it another eight hours and I could continue on my journey.

Chapter Three

Hidden History

I always thought change was good, but the more I read about what the world used to be like, the more I had to rethink my stance. Page after page of history seeped into my brain as I continued to search the Underground. Everything I believed about what the world was like prior to my personal memories was being challenged by the information before me. It was hard to believe that things happened so quickly, that change on such a large scale could take place over such a short period of time. I started to take down notes so I wouldn't forget any details. One of the things that Franklin warned me about was that information could be there one day, and disappear the next. If someone was caught posting to the Underground, there were severe consequences for them. The least of their worries was that their page would be taken down.

Based on what I discovered, the Climate Dissolution started approximately fifty years ago. It seems that people didn't believe that the world was experiencing something called climate change. Scientists tried to prove that the world was getting hotter, and that major problems would be coming if nothing were done. However, the majority just ignored what they said. I wish more people would have listened.

The temperature of the air started to increase over time. It wasn't something that people noticed right away, as it was a gradual thing. There was plenty of sunshine to enjoy, but if you wanted to spend your day outside, you had to check to see if the quality of the air was good enough for you to breathe in safely. If it wasn't, you had to grab your facemask before leaving the house. Some people couldn't afford to buy one, so they either had to stay inside, or risk it and suffer. There used to be ice in the seas that would reflect the heat from the sun, helping to cool the air. With the increased temperatures, the ice was melting everywhere, and the heat came on full force.

With the extra sunshine came more carbon dioxide. The world used to have more forests, more oceans, and more areas of dirt that would absorb these gases. With the ground becoming scorched, plant life was dying and the water sources were drying up. There wasn't a filtration system in nature anymore, and this led to people being forced to move from areas where the gases built up beyond the point where they could survive, even with masks.

The rise in temperatures was joined by more moisture in the air. This combination led to more hurricanes and tropical storms. Entire cities were destroyed in mere minutes, and nothing could be done to stop it. Over time, people learned that there was no point in rebuilding, as nature repeated its fury more than once in the same areas.

People tried to relocate, but help was limited, and most of them lost everything they had during these destructive times. It was hard for assistance to bring them relief, and citizens began to starve without proper food or water supplies. If they could manage to find sustenance, they might succumb to one of a variety of illnesses that plagued the areas due to the lack of clean conditions.

Families were always on the move, trying to escape what nature threw at them, but trouble was everywhere. Rising waters forced them to higher grounds, but there was only so much space to move to. Where there wasn't an issue with flooding, there was usually drought. Wildlife and plant life died out quickly, leaving no resources. The heat became so extreme, that people couldn't stay outside for more than minutes at a time. This made working conditions nearly impossible for some occupations, and certain careers became extinct.

With so much of the world uninhabitable, there was overcrowding in most areas. All borders between countries were gone, as there was no choice whether to allow individuals to come to places once their areas had been destroyed. People started to fight over food, water, and shelter. Everyday things became luxuries, and those who had access to them used their fortune to their advantage. Things such as public bathrooms became locked down, and you had to pay to use them. Nothing was free, as everyone fought to keep what they had, or make money by selling any excess of it. Greed was worse than it had ever been before.

Disorder was rampant, but small groups started coming together to try to organize ways to survive by helping one another. As each group was forming, they would choose a location where they could find the most supplies available to them. With these areas being so limited, several groups would find themselves in the same spots. Alliances were created, and smaller groups turned into larger ones. Over the course of a few years, these clusters started creating their own systems of leadership. Through various methods, they decided on who would be in charge, and which others would lead below them. Any semblance of the former governmental systems in the various countries had been overthrown much earlier on. These new leaders each worked on their areas, trying to keep their own little microcosms running smoothly.

Things were actually working out for a while as everyone came together in their own communities. However, with the conditions of the world continuing to get worse, the groups

41

found themselves starting to run out of supplies once again. There were no longer any new areas to explore, so the different sectors starting fighting with each other to take over the other one's domain. This took the small arguments that people were having previously and turned them into full-blown wars.

There was widespread bloodshed, as many people died during the fighting that took place. More regions were destroyed, limiting the supplies even further. Everyone realized that the current way of living wasn't going to last. If something were not done soon, the human race would be destroyed either directly or indirectly through lack of materials needed to survive. The leaders came together and decided that there needed to be one main leader to keep the others in check.

One man came to the minds of many people. He had been trying to work with his area leader and another one to smooth things over. He was one of the main citizens who were able to locate resources for food and water. He was good with his hands, able to help build things such as shelters when they were needed. His name was Apeiron, and it was decided that he would oversee the rest of the remaining humans in the world. The other leaders were split into four quadrants-Alpha, Beta, Gamma, and Delta. All citizens would be moved into one of those quadrants, and authority would be given out in various descending levels of a ruling system. A new world order was taking place, and people would do whatever it took to survive.

The quadrants were thriving as their citizens lived harmoniously among each other. Apeiron was maintaining a balance between the four areas, and the overseers (his team of leaders) helped within their individual districts. While the people of the world were learning how to live in peace, nature itself was still fighting against them. Food and water resources continued to struggle, and a decision was made that something else would have to be done to ensure the survival of humankind.

After many long discussions and gatherings, the leadership teams concluded that the biggest problem was that there were not enough means for all of the people. No matter how hard they tried, they could not balance the numbers. Since they couldn't increase the supplies, they would have to decrease the number of people who needed them. At first, limits were set in place for how many children each person would be allowed to have. The leaders figured that if they limited the amount of new mouths to feed coming into the world, then they could offer more supplies to those who were already struggling. This didn't work out, though, as women would have children in secret so that their numbers wouldn't show an increase. Safety and health hazards became an issue. Families who lost children in infancy begged to be allowed to try again. The system was flawed, and Apeiron knew it. Something else had to be done.

It seemed simple enough, but it took a lot of work before the answer finally came to them. If they couldn't prevent new children from being born, then they would have to end the existence of some of those people who were already living. Taking away people's lives would indeed lower the amount of people who used up what was already there. However, what would happen as new lives were born into the quadrants? There had to be a way to balance it all out, to make it even. Instead of just decreasing the current population, they would also have to focus on the amount of total lives at any given time. One life comes into existence, another one is taken out.

Apeiron instructed the quadrant leaders to take inventory of all of the citizens they had living in their area. Statistics such as age, identifying gender, and occupation were collected. It took some time, but eventually all of the data was gathered together into a large database, along with information on the average amount of new births each day. These facts allowed the leaders to see which members of society were the most valuable (in their opinions), and which were just taking up space (again, their opinions). Formulas were constructed using some of the top brains in each quadrant. Numbers were crunched, graphs were drawn up, and weeks were spent establishing the baseline. When all was said and done, the facts spoke for themselves. The numbers were chosen, and the death dates would be given out starting the first of the next month. With all of the time and effort it took to get the information together, you would think it would have taken a long time to come up with the method of execution that the overseers planned on using. That was not the case, though. The microchip was created rather quickly, and later on people would question how it came to be so fast.

Chapter Four

<u>Microchips</u>

Every life has a value, but how do we know what that is when it has only just begun? The overseers determined that best way to control the population would be to maintain a balance in the amount of people alive at any given time. By gathering all of the data on those who already existed in the world, they were able to determine how many people could remain based on what resources were currently available. Phase one was complete, and it was time to begin phase two.

The overseers needed to find a way to end a life without going around and simply killing people. They didn't want to be seen as murderers, but rather more as planners who were helping to keep a balance amongst the four quadrants. While working on a way to do this that was not violent or too horrific, the teams came up with the idea of the microchip.

This was intended to be a small device that would be implanted into the base of a person's medulla, at the bottom of the

47

brainstem, via injection by a needle. The placement guaranteed that any attempt at removal would automatically kill the person. The microchip would be encased in a small glass tube that is smaller than a grain of rice. Each chip would contain a GPS tracker, and would be able to be set off through radio frequency identification (RFID). The GPS would make it so that the overseers could tell where someone was at any given time. Using the RFID, they would be able to activate the chip when your time came. The chip would have a code on it that identified each particular person.

The dates were assigned so that the number of citizens alive would remain almost exactly the same at any given time. In the initial distribution, they set the death dates to take place during a greater spread of time, as they had no way of knowing how many new children would be born in the future, or how many people would die of other causes. As the days passed, the dates were given out based on how many people were supposed to be alive at that time. Each future child's assignment was determined by looking at how many people were going to be alive during its assumed lifetime. Then the team would figure out how long they could live before more babies would increase the numbers and throw everything off balance. It all came down to calculating the number of people versus the amount of resources available. It was a very scientific process, with no room for emotions.

The system was created so that all new children would receive their chip within hours of being born. It was a minor surgery, and would be done under the care of the doctor while still in the hospital. For those who were born outside of the hospital due to emergencies, the parents would have twenty-four hours to bring the child in and get their chip inserted. Home births were banned due to the lack of monitoring by the overseers that would take place. Every precaution was taken to make sure that no child escaped getting its chip.

Activation would take place by a signal that was sent via radio waves programmed to that particular number to trigger the self-destruct response. The reaction would trigger the glass to heat up, causing it to shatter and essentially cut the medulla so life functions would cease. If death did not occur instantly, it would ultimately happen within moments, caused by respiratory failure.

Once phase two started, the overseers needed to find a way to get the current citizens chipped. The leaders rounded everyone up by area and had their chips implanted through clinics that took place over several days. Since the procedure was considered a minor one, the people could go in, get it done, and then return home to rest after a while as their body healed. To ensure that everyone was complying, area leaders would go around to people's homes and do random checks. They would arrive with their hand scanners and check each person to certify that they did indeed have their chip. These checks were done periodically, and were never announced, so no one knew when someone might show up at their door.

Places of business were required to install scanners at all entrances that would check for people's chips as they came in. An alarm would go off if a body was detected without a chip, and it would immediately be sent to the local office to dispatch legal enforcement. There were cameras attached to all systems, so the image of the person would be caught as well. Finding a place to hide without being chipped would be very difficult.

Of course, there were people who would try to survive without allowing the overseers to implant them. They were nicknamed "Blanks", and there was no way to know how many of them existed. Usually it was a single person who tried to escape their fate, but occasionally you would find a family who attempted to make it on their own. The news was filled with stories of these people and their capture. The overseers loved to prove how they were in control. Whether you gave in and were implanted, or went on the run, you always lived in fear.

Even with the microchipping system in place, the overseers could not control people dying from other causes. Accidents and medical health issues still existed, and people would not always survive until their death date came around. That was what the GPS tracking system was for. Not only did it allow the overseers to know where you were at any given time, it also let them know if something happened to you.

There were teams of workers whose jobs were to strictly keep an eye on the trackers and their notifications. If someone died prior to their activation, a notification would show up and a worker would be sent to their last known location.

Once someone had died (whether activated or not), their body would be collected and sent to a facility run by the overseers to be cremated. Land space was limited due to the environmental conditions, so there were not enough places to bury the bodies. Family members were allowed to collect the remains, and services were still held to honor the deceased.

Knowing that you were constantly under the watchful eye of the overseers led some people to maintain a more active lifestyle, not wanting to waste any moment of their lives. For others, it brought them to the risky decision that they could do whatever they wanted, as they never knew when their life would end. There were still legal repercussions, and people would be sent to work camps to serve out sentences if they didn't follow the rules. The overseers didn't want to use death as a punishment, as it would throw off the numbers in their system. Having people work off their sentences for crimes they committed benefitted the citizens of the quadrants at the same time as punishing those who ignored the rules.

People did not agree with the concept of microchipping, but they didn't have a choice in the matter. The only thing you could do was hope that your date was set far off in the future. Parents feared for their children, and more people started planning for what might happen to them as the days went on. A big shift in people's attitudes was seen in the beginning, but as time went on, microchipping became just another part of life. When you can't change the future, why waste time worrying about it?

Chapter Five

<u>Becoming the Hacker</u>

My eyes opened to the stillness of the night. Immediately, Trixie sensed the shift in my sheets and came bounding over to me. Her breath was warm on my face, and I could still smell the hint of bacon that lingered from the biscuit I gave her right before bed. Slowly, I managed to drag my arm out from under my warm blanket, and the air instantly felt like ice shards against my skin. A glow appeared amongst the blackness, and I cringed as I looked down at my watch to see the time. It was only 3:34 a.m., an ungodly hour to be awake, especially when I knew that my alarm clock would be beeping at me in less than two hours.

The nightmares had been waking me up almost every night, and sucking whatever energy might be left out of my normally worn out body. All I wanted was one night where I could sleep and then wake up the next morning feeling rested. Visions of my father dying, my mother hysterically crying, and my sister's face as she aged over the last thirteen years have been flashing in my brain every time I closed my eyes. Solid sleep escaped me, seemingly just out of my reach. I tried to bundle back up, but Trixie wasn't having it. She started yipping at me, insistent that she needed to go out now that I appeared to be awake. Wrapping the blanket around me, I begrudgingly lifted myself out of bed and headed to the back door. "Be quick, girl", I told her as I slid open the door and braced myself for the frost. It was rare to have the temperature drop so low, and my body was not ready for it. I squinted my eyes to try and follow her as she ran to the back of the yard to do her business. She returned and waited for me to let her back in. The cold blast of air on my face was just enough to start my brain going. So much for going back to sleep.

Flicking on the kitchen light, I shielded my eyes as they tried to adjust to the change in brightness. It was too early to eat breakfast, but my stomach was rumbling now that I was up and moving around. Even though I didn't really want to eat, my body had other plans. I dug through the pantry and decided upon a bag of protein cheese crisps. They may not have been the healthiest choice, but they weren't too heavy and would do for the moment. Making my way to the living room, I sat down on the couch and called for Trixie to join me. She immediately jumped up and spun around a few times before settling in next to me. Those moments made me glad I took her in last year. I wasn't sure if I would be able to handle a pet on my own with my work hours, but she is a really well trained dog. I can be gone for eight hours and I don't even need to keep her in the crate anymore.

I turned on the television, flipping through the various channels to try to find something to stimulate my mind. Nothing good was on that early in the morning, so I resigned myself to watching some show on how to make a beautiful five-course meal on a limited budget. Once in a while I tossed Trixie a cheese crisp, as both of us sat there passing the time until the day officially began. Eventually five thirty rolled around, signaling that it was time to get ready for work.

Every day basically started the same way for me. My alarm would go off and I kind of oozed out of bed. I have never been a morning person, so it was a struggle to get up and get moving. Peeling off my clothes, I started with a shower to help and try to wake my brain up. It never worked, but at least I was clean. Brushed my teeth, fixed my hair, and grabbed a pair of jeans along with one of my many shirts with our company's logo on it. I was glad we were allowed to dress comfortably for work; it made it easier to sit at my desk for eight hours when I didn't feel constricted by my clothes. Eating early in the morning always made me feel nauseous, so I just prepared myself some coffee to take with me and grabbed a protein bar. I was out the door by 6:15, and it was only a fifteen-minute drive to work, getting me there right on time each day. One of the reasons I originally chose to work there was because I could be done with my day by 3:30, which got me home in time to help my mom out with Davina. It wasn't a planned thing at first, as I was happy to have moved out and had time for myself. However, I was able to see that my mom needed me, so I found myself spending more time over at their place in the afternoons. Every time I would try to pull myself away more, I kept hearing dad's words reverberating in my ear. Davina was my little sister, and she was my responsibility. When it got to be too much for me, I focused more on my job, adding extra hours in to hang out with the coders and learn more about what they did.

***

Suddenly five years had passed without much fanfare. It was hard to believe that I had been working for Prothymos for so long. I felt like I had learned so much while at the company, but there was always so much more to understand. I was writing my own code, and some other person got to catch my mistakes. That part was a lot harder than I thought it would be, but it was also a lot more fun. I was still the grunt of the team, as the people I worked with had many more years' experience than I did when it came to actually writing code. For the most part, I bounced my ideas off them, and they helped me figure out how to improve them. Then they rejected them, and I tried again. It sounds cruel, but I did appreciate how honest they were with me. Some of my team members have their names attached to a few high rated games in the industry. They have been in my position before, and have worked their way up to where they currently were. I respected the totem pole, even if I was on the bottom.

The more I learned about coding, the more I started finding other areas of computing that piqued my interest. After Franklin showed me the world of the Underground a few years ago, I gained knowledge that very few people had access to, or even knew existed. Every spare moment that I had went to diving deeper and deeper. Some files had messages stating they no longer existed, or were corrupt. I had to wonder how much truth was behind that. Even with things being shared in the Underground, were there still limits to what I could get into? I was determined to find a way to make sure I saw it all, so I turned my focus to the crazy and dangerous world of hacking.

It wasn't something that I had planned on doing, it just sort of happened out of frustration. The Underground appeared to be limitless, so when something would get in my way, I wanted to find a way to get through it, not just around it. What made those little trips even more interesting was that in order to learn how to hack my way *through* the Underground, I had to find resources that were only available to me via the Underground. You would think that the odds were stacked against me, but strangely enough, that wasn't the case. There was plenty of information available to me; it just took some extra digging around to find it. While I knew there were ways to communicate with others during my searches, I didn't feel comfortable regarding this. There were legal boundaries that I was crossing, and anonymity only goes so far when you're still learning how to cover your tracks.

I spent a lot of time doing my research, using every spare moment I could gather to track down as much information as possible. It was difficult to try to remember so much, but I was too scared to keep a notebook in case anyone might come across it. Once I felt that I had enough knowledge on how to hack a system, I attempted my first break.

I didn't want to try anything too big to start with, so my first official hack was my own phone. Jailbreaking it so I could add on extra apps wasn't a difficult thing to do. The success of something even so minor fueled my fire. I wanted to go bigger, and see if I could do something that had the possibility of affecting others. Using email as my target, I did a little phishing into the accounts of the local university. That was definitely harder than the phone, but I found my way through the system without any real problems. I did a little snooping, but didn't really mess with anyone or their content. These hacks were not about doing damage, they were to push myself and see how much I knew and understood. It was so hard not to tell anyone what I was doing, but I knew that if I wanted to continue with it, I couldn't trust somebody with my secret. I tried a few more small hacks, then figured it was time to go big.

The scale had to be large enough to see if I was truly capable of pulling it off, but I didn't want to be crazy and go for something dangerous like a bank. I ended up deciding to go with Sahara, the largest online merchant out there. I used a method referred to as password spraying to gain access. That allowed me to have to only come up with a single password that would be pitted against all of the users in their system. While many people have learned not to use basic passwords that would be so obvious to the average person, there are always one or two who just don't listen. Those people were the weak links that I was looking for, relying on their lack of adherence to the rules to allow me an entryway into the system.

It wasn't long before the spraying had worked, when another obstacle hit me. They used multi-factor authentication, and I had to figure out the answer to the next question. Thankfully, I was able to quickly get through that as well, seeing as to how the person continued to foolishly use common information that I could guess in mere seconds. That was it, I had made it in! There wasn't anything that I really wanted to do to hurt their system; I was mostly just testing out if I was even capable of getting in or not. I didn't want to stay on there too long, as I was concerned that I might be caught. I still had a lot more knowledge to gain in order to fully feel comfortable with manipulating the data I was accessing. I did some quick searches while logged in to see what I could find, and then shut everything down on my end.

My heart was racing to the beat of a hundred racehorses running 'round the track as I thought about what I had just done. I was beyond exhilarated, but my enthusiasm was tempered by my worry of what would happen if I were found out. I had not done any damage to their networks, so I wasn't sure what the extent of the crime was that I had just committed. Yes, it was still wrong, but at least I didn't hurt anyone or do any damage to Sahara's institution.

What I *did* do, was prove to myself that I could hack a pretty big system. It was an amazing feeling, knowing that I could accomplish a feat that I had been working towards for quite some time. I wanted to scream, shout, and tell everyone I knew, but that wasn't going to happen for obvious reasons. Instead, I poured myself a drink, put my feet up, and tried to capture the moment in my memories so I would never forget it.

When I went back to work, I was expecting to hear everyone talking about what had happened to Sahara's network. Shockingly, not a word was spoken about it. Of course, I couldn't be the one to bring it up, as that would be suspicious. I waited all day, but there was not one mention of it. It bugged me my entire shift, and continued to bother me once I was back home. Why was no one speaking about the break in? Did I imagine the whole thing? It picked at my brain all night, until I finally fell asleep.

The next morning, I awoke once again to my alarm, right on time. I opened my eyes in time to see Trixie dashing towards my bed, tongue lolling out of her mouth as she approached me. I couldn't help but smile as I saw her. Walking towards the shower, my brain started to replay the previous day, still trying to figure out what went wrong. That was when I began to understand. Nothing was wrong; I had pulled it off without a hitch. No one was talking about it because I had done it right. I wasn't sure if the people at Sahara would realize that someone had broken in or not, but since I didn't change anything, there was nothing to talk about. I did what I had set out to do. A goal was set, and I had managed to achieve it. All of the time that I had spent learning what to do, and the job itself was completed from start to finish in just a few minutes' time. As excited as I had been to do it in the first place, now that it was done, I was feeling a bit of a letdown. There was only one way to get back that initial feeling. As any addict must do, it was time to up the ante.

Chapter Six

Download and Disseminate

The desire to pull off another hack was gnawing within me. I wanted to feel that thrill once again, to know I could reach inside a network and see things I shouldn't be seeing. Hacking became like a drug to me, and I needed my fix. Only this time, I wanted to choose a location that had personal meaning. If I was going to risk everything with the possibility of getting caught, I required a reason behind the system break in. It was time to plunge through barriers. To not only check out the information, but to have a little bit of fun with it, too. I was ready to push it to the next level.

Time was flying by with the way I kept myself so busy trying to learn as much as I could about computer hacking. While scrolling through my calendar to check on upcoming plans, I had the embarrassing realization that I had almost forgotten about Davina's upcoming birthday! My little sister was growing up so fast, and I didn't want to miss any part of her life. Now that I wasn't spending as much time with her, I wanted to make sure special days were fully honored. She was getting too old to have a traditional birthday party, but the family would be getting together to celebrate. Not being sure what to get her, I decided to give her a call and ask her what she was interested in.

"Hey, I was just checking in to see if there was anything special you wanted for your birthday."

"Well, what I really want is a puppy, but mom has made it very clear that I won't be getting one."

"That sucks, but I get it. You are always welcome to come visit me and play with Trixie. She would love to see you, and she can never get enough belly rubs." I laughed as I pictured the last time Davina was at my house. It seemed like forever ago, and I really wished she could come by more often.

"I just might have to take you up on that offer. I'll talk to mom and see what we can plan. It's been too long." Just like that, she read my mind.

"That's for sure. So, any other ideas on what I can get you, or will it be another gift card kind of celebration?" I wasn't known for having the best ideas when it came to giving presents, so gift cards usually sufficed in a pinch.

"Whatever you want is fine. Just having you here will be the best present you can give me." It sounded cheesy, but I knew that she meant it.

"You're no help. I'll be there, and I'll try and be creative with my contribution to honoring your special day."

We chatted for a bit longer about how things were going in school for her (doing great), and how she was getting along with mom (not as great). It was nice to catch up, and I focused on remembering to do that more often. It wasn't that I didn't think about my family, it's just that I was so busy with work and learning about hacking skills that I tended to push everything else aside.

Davina's birthday always held a special place in my heart. It was impossible to forget the remarkable moments of that day-when she entered the world, and when our father left it. My brain played a tug of war each year as it tried to celebrate Davina and mourn the passing of my dad. It was a moment in time I struggled with annually. It was while thinking about all of the years that had passed, each birthday/death day, when it came to me. I knew exactly what I was going to use my hacking skills on next.

***

Ever since the microchipping had begun over twenty years ago, the overseers have kept a database with all of the information on every citizen in it. They have the person's name, date of birth, and their assigned death dates. Each file also has other details in it, such as their GPS tracking location data and their given code to activate their microchip. I wasn't interested in that extraneous information, though. I just wanted to know what death dates people had been given. How many lives could be changed if people knew when they were supposed to die? If my mother knew my father was going to die right around when his child would have been born, would she have continued with the pregnancy?

Would knowing your future cause you to try to change it? The day that Apeiron implemented the microchip to have power over population control, people knew that their death date was predetermined. The concept of leaving things up to fate simply did not exist anymore. Sure, there were always things that could happen that might kill you before your assigned time, but you still knew that the overseers could end your life whenever they wanted to. There was an underlying fear that existed in every citizen in the four quadrants. What would happen if they had the opportunity to find out when their time was supposed to be up? Would everyone want to know?

It didn't take much for me to conclude that this would have to be my next project. It wasn't so much a choice as an assignment. I, Adelaine Kingston, would find out the death dates of everyone in the four quadrants. After my success with the Sahara hack, I felt confident that I could get into a network without being seen. However, I had to work out the kinks when it came to actually downloading the files that had all of the data on them. It was time to go for a ride in the Underground.

The first thing I needed to do was to locate exactly where the files were kept. Various sites led me in different directions, so I had to weed out the incorrect information and filter it all down to a basic outline. It appeared that each quadrant kept information on their own citizens, but then those databases were collected and fed into a main one that Apeiron could control. It made life easier for him, to have access to it all in one place. It also made it easier for me.

I decided that using the same method of password spraying that I had used previously on Sahara wouldn't be the best way to get in this time. One of the other techniques that I had learned was the File Transfer Protocol (FTP) method. If I could get access to one of the system programmer's log-ins that works with the database, then I could drop a key logger and just wait for them to log in. That got my foot in the door, so to speak. Then I could get into the files where the death dates were saved, and snatch a copy of them. Since I would be logging in using their credentials, it wouldn't appear that anyone else had gone in and disrupted things. I would be a stealthy ninja from behind the screen.

The level of difficulty in getting that done was greater than I had anticipated, especially since it was so much easier to get into Sahara's systems. Still, I was fiercely determined, and I managed to get everything ready to go. My firewall was set up, and I had multiple layers and changes in place for my VPNs. With a few mouse clicks, I suddenly had the numbers appearing on my computer. In less than one hour, I was able to see when every citizen was assigned to die.

My immediate thought was to look up everyone I knew and see what their file said. I stopped myself, though, as I wasn't sure if that was information that I truly wanted to know. I grew up knowing that everyone around me had a death date, myself included. I watched my own father die suddenly when his microchip was activated on the day my little sister was born. What would I do differently, if anything, once I knew when my loved ones were going to die? I held what could arguably be considered some of the most important information in the world in my hands, and I was scared to look at it.

I decided to try to sleep that night without having made the decision about what to do with the copy of the database yet. I tossed and turned, Trixie standing guard below me, confused as to what was going on. After a couple of hours, I knew there was no way I was going to be able to get any rest until I had made a final decision.

***

Several warm droplets of water pooled on my shoulders as the rest made their way down my body and into the drain at the bottom of the shower. I stood there until the water turned cold, trying to wrap my head around what I had done, and what steps I would take next. I had planned every step to get the figures, but I had not worked out the particulars when it came to what I wanted to do with them. I felt a heavy weight throughout my body, dragging me down as if every number was pressing against my skin. The only way to unburden myself was to share the weight with others.

As I toweled off and put on some fresh clothing, I engaged Trixie in a one-way conversation while attempting to work out all of my thoughts. She happily obliged me, following me back and forth while I paced throughout the house. When I came to a conclusion, I jumped onto the couch and grabbed my laptop. I wasn't sure what I wanted to do for myself with all of this information, but perhaps others might know what *they* would do with it. I didn't need to take on everyone else's problems, but I was going to give in this one time and let them take on mine. The database was not my weight to bear alone. Everyone knew it existed, and now they were about to find out how to get into it.

Chapter Seven

Sharing the Wealth

My next step had to be figuring out a way to let people know that this information was now available to them. I was worried that if I just gave it away to everyone, there would be dreadful circumstances that might arise. There needed to be a selection process, some way to narrow it down so that only people who really wanted to find out their death dates would be able to. Those who wanted to stay in the dark would not be forced to see the light. I tried to think of various ways to figure out who might want to know and who wouldn't, but I could never pinpoint exactly how to come to those conclusions. Every time I thought about a reason why someone in particular might want to know, I would always come up with a reason why they wouldn't and vice versa. I surmised that the decision had to be made by each individual, not by me. I was going to make the data available, but the people had to choose whether or not they wanted to find it out.

The easiest and quickest way to get news out had always been to post it on social media sites. People loved to find the newest thing and share it with everyone they knew. It was like a competition, whoever got a hold of the latest "hot" story first got the equivalent of cool points. I knew that if I created enough buzz about it, all I would have to do is get the story out there, and let everyone else do the work of spreading it for me. The hard part was creating all new accounts that didn't lead back to me so that my identity remained a secret. I had to start with the basics and then build from there so that every step along the way was protected. It wasn't too hard of a challenge, but it was majorly time consuming.

I spent several hours developing a character that would exist solely in the online world. Tossing around a bunch of different names, I couldn't think of one that seemed like a fun way to capture the essence of what I had done. In the end, I decided to just go by Hacker. Not the most creative name, but it was easy to remember, and right to the point of what this person was supposed to be. Developing accounts for every outlet I could think of, I was ready to put my message out there.

It was easier for people to reach out to me than for me to try to contact them, so I had set up an untraceable messaging account where others could write to me. The hardest part was figuring out how I would determine who would get their death dates. Did I just give them to anyone who contacted me? Should I do some sort of lottery that people entered? With information this sensitive, I wanted to make it a little more difficult for people to get it. After all, I was putting my entire existence on the line by hacking into that database, and I deserved some recognition for it, even if it wasn't really me that was getting it. Since I couldn't let people know who I was, I figured that the best way to feel like I was going to get something out of this was to ask for financial compensation.

Setting the price tag on a death date was not an easy process. It was determining how much someone's life was worth, and I didn't feel comfortable doing that. There was a game of ping-pong going on inside my brain, and the bouncing of the ball was giving me a headache. Too low of a value, then anyone could just get them, and their worth would drop. Too high, and no one would get them, making all of this work a waste of time. I also wasn't sure how I was going to handle it if too many people reached out to me all at once, since it was going to be a delicate process to send the information without being caught. I eventually decided that the cost to purchase a death date would be fifty thousand dollars. That would make it so that most people would have to find a way to get the money, and I wouldn't be inundated with requests. It also helped me weed out anyone who was just going to try to find me to turn me in.

Setting up an account where the money would be sent to was more difficult, but not impossible. Of course, it had to be done through a different quadrant, making it appear that I was living somewhere further away than I actually was. Thanks to the Underground, I found a way to set up a ghost account that was untraceable. Payments would be made online through transfers, and no one would ever see me in person.

I needed to come up with the perfect message to post so that people would be curious, and would be tempted to find out if what I was saying was legitimate or not. An incentive would be needed, as everyone loves to get something for free. Giving away a few dates should be enough to get people talking, so I decided that I would offer it at no charge to the first five people who got in contact with me. Then I had to hope that they would spread the word so that others would want a piece of the action.

After much deliberation, I created a short and simple message to go out:

I have a copy of the Death Dates database. If you want to find out what yours is, contact me at the account listed with the information requested below. The first five people to reach me will get theirs FREE. After that, it will be at a cost of $50,000 per date. This is NOT a joke. Do you want to know when you will die? I can tell you!

At the bottom of the message, I included the account information that would allow them to get a hold of me. I also included some questions that would give me enough information to determine who each person was in case of duplicate names. The last thing I needed would be to send someone the wrong death date. I took a deep breath and hit send. I did it again and again as I posted the same message on each platform. It wouldn't be long before I got my first message back.

"Hey Hacker! I am pretty sure this is some kind of joke, but I figured it wouldn't hurt to try it anyway. So here goes nothing! I would like to find out my death date. My name is Roscoe Knight, and you can reach me at this mail account. I hope I am one of the first five, since I am basically broke and could never afford the $50,000 to buy it otherwise. Still doubting this is real, but here I am writing anyway. Thanks!"

Roscoe may not have believed in what I was doing, but they were smart to write to me so quickly, as they were not only one of the first five, they were number one. I wrote them back immediately and sent them the link they would need to get their death date. Once Roscoe opened my message, they would see nothing but a link. Once they clicked on that, the process would begin that would take them to their death date. It was all pretty quick, and the information would disappear from the screen relatively fast so that there was no trace. I didn't want to use a bunch of special effects or anything to make it look too cheesy. It needed to make people pay attention, and leave them with their thoughts once they received the numbers. I was proud of how I had set it all up. Of course, I had no way to know what would happen once they opened their message, as I made it so that they couldn't get back in touch with me after I had responded. The account I had for people to contact me at was only a forwarding one that went to various temporary set ups. Once I wrote them back, that account was gone, and any messages they tried to send to it would kick back. Just one more way to prevent tracing of who I truly was.

The next four people who I got messages from came in within minutes. I did the same process with each of them, locating their death dates and sending them the link. It was invigorating to know that I was getting the information out there, but also extremely frustrating to not know what people were thinking. Now that the first five people had been contacted, it was time to try to start making some money. This was either going to make me rich, or be a big bust. It was time to find out. I posted another message in the same outlets I had posted before as a sort of follow up.

This is the Hacker. I have already received and fulfilled the requests from five people. I have a copy of the Death Dates database. If you want to find out what yours is, contact me at the account listed with the information requested below. The cost is $50,000 per date. This is NOT a joke. Do you want to know when you will die? I can tell you!

I went back and looked at my original posts to see what kinds of responses people had left on them. It was amazing how many comments were there so fast! Of course, there were tons of doubters, which I had expected. Many people were asking for proof, which I really didn't have a way of providing. I did my part with the first five people, and it was now up to them to decide what they wanted to do with what I gave them.

***

I decided to occupy my time with other things for a while, allowing the citizens of the four quadrants to (hopefully) spread my message for me. My stomach was grumbling, so I decided to go out and grab a bite to eat. It was a beautiful day that led to me stopping at a little café that had an outdoor eating area. I sat at a small table with my tray and soaked in the sunshine. I tried to get lost in my thoughts, but kept finding myself tuning into the conversations of those around me. There was a couple discussing an upcoming vacation, a family trying to wrangle the kids to sit and eat, and some college kids talking about what classes they needed to finish up to get their degrees.

I was enjoying myself, nibbling at the variety of flavors I was eating, when suddenly a small group walked outside. They were chattering away very enthusiastically, when I overheard the words *death dates*, *hacker,* and *fifty thousand dollars.* No. Freaking. Way. I turned my ears to what they were saying, and heard a discussion about the posts I had made.

A couple of the people didn't believe it was true, but the others were saying that it sounded like something that could be real. They were arguing amongst themselves when something was said that made me almost choke on the bite I was chewing.

"If it's fake, then how do you explain the post made by that girl saying that she was one of the first five?" one of them responded to the ongoing debate.

"She probably just wanted some sort of celebrity status. Claiming that she is part of this elusive group of people makes others talk about her. Prime example." With that remark, one of the people pointed to the original speaker.

"Okay, but just imagine that it *is* real for a second. Wouldn't it be cool to find out your death date?"

"I don't know, it all seems…" That was the last bit that I was able to capture, as they group walked off towards the parking lot.

I couldn't believe my ears, they were talking about it! I grabbed my phone from my pocket and began scrolling through the various sites to see what was being said. It had worked, the posts were blowing up! I wanted to rush home so I could take more time to read through everything, so I shoved the last few bites in my mouth and headed out. On the way home, I realized that I was in desperate need of groceries, consequently forcing me to make a quick stop at the grocery store. Keeping my pace up, I was able to get through the aisles quickly since there weren't many people shopping at that time. It was in line where I heard another person talking about the big news. They were chatting up the cashier, as most people tend to do while waiting on their purchases to be rung up.

"Did you hear about this Hacker and how they got a hold of the Death Dates info?" the older gentleman in front of me asked the young woman who was scanning his items.

"I've been working all day, but I have had several people mention it. I wonder how they got into the system."

"I don't know, but they must be both brilliant and really stupid. Can you imagine what would happen to them if they were caught? The overseers would probably torture them before killing them." The man seemed just a bit too enthusiastic over that last part and I was getting uncomfortable standing behind him.

"I don't even know whether or not to believe it. There are some crazies out there, that's for sure." She gave him his total, and with that, the man got his cart and walked away.

"I couldn't help but overhear your conversation with that guy. This whole thing does seem a little weird, doesn't it?" I really wanted to get more information out of her, to see what people had to say about what I had done.

"It's definitely weird. I mean, I wouldn't mind knowing my date, but I highly doubt I could get my hands on $50,000. It's not like I make a lot working here, and I'm trying to save up for school." She seemed to be a few years younger than I was, and she had her goals laid out in front of her. "I really want to be a nurse, but all of those classes are so expensive. I'm saving some money living at home now, but I'm also trying to help my mom out with the bills, so I can't put away as much as I'd like to."

"It's awesome that you have plans already. I am sure things will work out for you. I believe that what you put out into the universe comes back to you tenfold. You seem like a good person, so you should have a lot of great things coming to you." She thanked me and handed me my receipt. I said goodbye and walked away feeling a tinge of guilt.

Was I putting good out into the universe by doing this? Offering people the chance to find out their dates by making them pay money that they might not have. What kind of karmic retribution might that bring me? I had to stop worrying about it; I had made up my mind already after a lot of deep thought. Now was not the time to doubt myself.

***

As I opened my front door, Trixie trotted up between my legs, almost making me drop my bags. I leaned down and gave her a quick pet, and then put the bags on the table. All I could think about was how people were reacting. The names of the first five were swirling through my head. Now that they had their answers, what would they do with the information? I knew it was the right way to handle things, but I kind of hated myself for cutting off all communication with them. Now I had no way of finding out what the results of their inquests would be. It was like mailing someone a present that you knew they really wanted, and never getting to see the look on their face when they open it.

Once I had put away all of my groceries, I grabbed my laptop and made myself comfortable on the couch. Trixie brought me her big chewy bone to play fetch with, but I was too focused on the task at hand. After a few nudges at my hand with her head, she realized that I wasn't going to give in and settled on laying down next to me instead. I logged into my first account, not even having to do a search before I found remarks just popping up on my screen. There were so many comments out there, so many people who were talking about what I had done.

One of the posts stood out to me, as it was very short and simple. All it had was the word PROOF written on it, followed by a link. I have always been hesitant to follow links that I didn't know, but the address of this one included the words database and Hacker in it. Of course, I had no choice but to click on it. When I did, I was taken to a page from one of the news networks. My jaw dropped as I read the heading of the story: *Overseers Confirm Breach of Death Dates Database*. There it was for everyone to see, the proof that I needed to let people know what I was did was real. Reading the article, I learned that the overseers had decided to confirm that someone named the Hacker had indeed broken into their database and gotten a copy of the death dates. They emphasized that they would find the person or persons responsible and would punish them severely. The story was brief, but concluded by saying that they didn't have any current leads, and the overseers were offering $250,000 to anyone who could identify who the Hacker was.

This shit was getting real. All security measures had been taken to make sure that I couldn't be traced back to the breach in their system. My set-up for getting the information to those who requested it was also as secure as I could make it. Still, I had to worry that someone might be able to figure out who I was. With a bounty of such a high amount on my head now, people would be more interested in solving the puzzle. All safety precautions would have to be checked and rechecked regularly to ensure my protection.

I continued to search through the rest of the posts, but it became overwhelming as more and more people were talking about it. It seemed that every time I read what someone had written, another person would put something up. The conversation was flowing at a pace that was just too much for me to keep up with. My eyes were watering, so I got up and went to get a drink while taking a break from staring at my screen. After gulping down the refreshing coldness and making a stop at the bathroom, I returned to my spot on the couch. I decided that I couldn't handle reading any more about myself for the moment, and went to open my email instead.

Scanning each subject line, I found that most of what was in my mailbox was junk. Then there was this one: *Death Date Request-Payment Enclosed*. Of course, it wasn't addressed to me; it had been forwarded through my hidden account and was addressed to the Hacker. I hesitated just a moment before clicking on it. In front of me was a message from a woman named Winnifred. She didn't write much, just that she would like her death date, and she included all of the information that I needed to determine who she was so I could get it to her. Just as she stated in her subject line, the payment had been sent. I checked my account, and it was there, all fifty thousand dollars. My heart started racing as I realized that all of the work I had done was finally paying off. Even if no one else reached out to me, I already had more money now than I had ever had before in my lifetime.

This woman believed me, and now I was going to change her life forever. I gathered up her numbers and sent her the link to take her to the information. No turning back now. When I sent the messages to the first five, I didn't feel the same way. I guess because no money was exchanged, it didn't seem quite as real. They could choose to believe what I showed them or not. It wasn't going to make that much of a difference since they didn't have anything invested in their request. When it came to Winnifred, she was paying me a lot of money to get her death date. She had an absolute interest in getting her numbers, and was willing to spend a large amount to get them. I felt more of a responsibility to her than I had to the other five. It was done, and once again, I had no way of knowing what would happen on her end once she opened up my message. I hoped for the best, and mentally walked away.

***

I wasn't sure how many more, if any, would reach out to me. I was excited at the prospect of the money coming in, but was fully aware that I was at risk each day that I continued to do this. I decided that I needed to choose a stopping point. That would allow me a peace of mind, knowing that I would only be doing this for a set amount of time and could then move on. It also let every citizen know that they didn't have forever to make their decision as to whether or not they would reach out to me. The viral spread of my message took over quickly, so I was hoping that I would be hearing from more people relatively soon. After some internal debate, I decided upon one month as my timeline. I would give everyone just one month to come up with the money and contact me if they wanted to know their death date.

The deadline was set, and the waiting game had begun. The next day I would check my mailbox and see another request. Then another. And another. A change was coming, and I was bringing it.

Part Two

Actions

Chapter Eight

Eloise & Julian

The incessant beeping and clicking from the machines was giving me a headache. On the other hand, it could have been from the medication that was slowly dripping into my veins. Perhaps it was from the constant conversation that my husband insisted on having just to fill the time. I appreciated him being there with me, but sometimes I wished he would had agreed to stay home. It was only four hours, and I had a collection of books I still needed to read. He just always came across as being so awkward there. He couldn't be comfortable, his chair was much harder than the comfortable ones they let the patients relax on as we received the chemicals. Yet he came with me, week after week, all because he loved me.

***

It was just two months from when we were getting ready to celebrate six years of having been married, but we have been together for almost eleven years. Having met in art school, we talked about how we both dreamed of traveling through the quadrants. Neither one of us wanted to have any kids, so we were unencumbered to just go where our dreams would steer us. We wanted to take it all in, and then put it back out through our various mediums. Julian's focus was on painting, while I was majoring in sculpture. He swept me off my feet on our first date when instead of bringing me flowers, he brought me a framed painting of roses that he had made just for me (at least, that's what he told me). It took five years of dating before he finally asked me to marry him. All of my friends and family questioned why I stayed with him so long without a ring, but I knew he was the one I wanted to be with, so I was willing to wait. Our core beliefs lined up with each other, we shared similar interests in movies and books. He made me laugh, and even more importantly, he got my twisted sense of humor. We were young, and the world laid at our feet. We had big plans, but life got in the way.

As my thirtieth birthday loomed on the horizon, I started getting pains in my abdomen a lot. At first, the doctors all told me it was just stress about hitting the big three-oh. I had a history of heartburn, so I was given a prescription for some meds to help reduce stomach acid, and was sent on my way. My appetite had decreased and I was losing weight, but since I was overweight, the doctors joked about how I had found an easy diet to follow. Nothing seemed to be seriously wrong, and all of the physicians were telling me I was fine, so I believed them.

Julian had planned a big celebration for my special day. He had hired a stretch limousine to pick us up, then stop and get several friends along the way to the restaurant. Once we got there, more friends joined us in the reserved back room to enjoy some delicious food and indulge in too many drinks. During the ride to the restaurant, my stomach really started to hurt. I guess I wasn't too great at hiding my pain, as Julian obviously noticed something was wrong.

"Eloise, are you feeling okay? You look a little pale."

"My belly hurts, but I'm sure it's just a little motion sickness. I'll be fine."

"Try and look out the window, maybe that will help. We should be there soon. I'm sorry; I just wanted to make this night exceptional for you. Your thirtieth birthday should be one you always remember."

"Don't be sorry, babe. This is not your fault. Don't worry; I'm sure it will go away once I get out of the limo and can sit still for a bit."

Shortly after arriving at the restaurant, I had already started to feel much better. By the time the food started coming out, my appetite was back and I was looking forward to what was to come. Dinner was fantastic, and each course was even better than the one that preceded it. The sommelier came in and recommended which wines paired well with each plate. I ate and drank so much more than I should have, and my body was less than thrilled with me. Before the night was over, I was on my knees in the women's restroom, promising never to drink again if someone could just make it stop. Julian had sent in a friend to check on me, and I told her between heaves to let him know that I would be fine. After about twenty minutes, I finally felt well enough to reappear at my own party. It was late, and several people had left while I was indisposed.

"Hey, welcome back! Had a little bit too much of the birthday fun?" Julian was making light of the situation, but I could see the look of concern in his eyes.

"Yeah, too much food, too much drink, it was all too much for a thirty year old, I guess."

Julian gave me a gentle squeeze and kissed my forehead. We paraded around the room together, chatting it up with people until the only ones left were the ones that arrived with us.

"Are you going to be okay to ride back in the limo? How are you feeling?"

"I'm still in pain, but I should be alright. I'm so sleepy, I'm just going to try and lie down on the way home."

I passed out shortly after we pulled away from the restaurant, and didn't wake up until Julian was carrying me into the house. I felt badly for not saying goodbye to our friends as we dropped them off, but those glasses of wine had really done me in. Julian laid me down on the bed, and started to undress me so I could sleep more comfortably. I remember him placing the blanket over me, but then it was lights out until morning.

The sun came up the next day, and I quickly remembered how I had a project to finish that someone had consigned. It was a rather expensive piece, and I couldn't allow myself to get behind on it. I sat up in bed, and cried out in pain. Julian was still asleep, but my wailing woke him up instantly. The pain was so intense, I couldn't move.

"Julian, something's wrong," I sobbed as tears flowed freely down my face.

"Okay, let's head to the emergency room. Do you think you can make it to the car, or do I need to call an ambulance?"

"I don't think I can move."

Julian threw on some clothes as he grabbed his phone and called for help. He gathered some clothes for me, but it hurt too much to try to put them on. He tossed them in a bag and waited as he sat beside me on the bed.

"They're on their way. We'll get this figured out. Just hang in there, okay?"

"Is this what getting old is supposed to feel like?" I tried to crack a smile, but everything hurt.

The sirens got louder as they approached the apartment. Julian ran to the door when he heard the first knock, and led the medics to the back bedroom. They took some vitals and asked me a bunch of questions before loading me onto the stretcher. As they raised my body onto the platform, I let out a howl like an injured wolf. When I heard it, I found it hard to believe that the sound was actually emanating from my own body. At some point, I passed out from the pain, because the next thing I remembered, I was in the hospital.

An IV was placed in my left hand, which was providing me with some electrolytes to balance out those that I had lost the night before from being sick. My head was foggy, and I was having a hard time focusing, but I wasn't in pain. If nothing else, I was thankful for that. My mouth was dry when I tried to speak, and my throat felt a little sore.

"Hey, look who's waking up!" Julian said to me as my eyelids fluttered open. "You're in the hospital, but it's okay. Do you remember what happened?"

"My stomach", I barely managed to squeak out.

"Does it hurt? Do you need more pain medication? I can call for the nurse..."

"No, it's okay. Is that why I'm here?" I had vague memories of the pain from earlier, but most of the morning was a blur.

"Yes, your stomach was hurting you a lot, and we had to call an ambulance. They have run some tests on you, and now we're just waiting for the results. Do you need anything?"

"Just some water. My mouth is really dry."

Julian stepped out for a minute and walked over to the nurse's station to see if he could get me something to drink. When he returned, he told me that the nurse said I was only allowed ice chips, and she would be bringing me a cup of them in a minute. I really wanted something to drink, but I guess that would have to do.

As I let each chunk of frozen water slowly dissolve in my mouth, I started to get sleepy again from the pain medications that were coursing through my veins. I was having a hard time keeping my eyes open, so I decided to stop fighting against them and went back to sleep. I drifted off to the sounds of the television intermingled with the beeping of the machines in my room.

***

I wasn't sure how much time had passed during my nap, but when I opened my eyes, no one else was in the room this time. Still not entirely sure of what was going on; I reached for the red button and called the nurse. She came in just a few moments later, and told me that the doctor would be coming in to see me now that I was awake again. Wondering where Julian was, I was about to ask the nurse if she had seen him when he joined us in the room suddenly.

"Hey, sorry I wasn't here when you woke up. I had to get some caffeine and sugar." He held up a hot drink container and a couple of candy bars, then placed them on a side table and sat down. The nurse asked if I needed anything, and then left the room when I told her I was okay.

"The nurse told me that the doctor will be coming to see me. Did they tell you anything?" For the first time, Julian avoided my eyes. I got an immediate sense that something was wrong. Like a teenager who just got caught drinking by their parents, I immediately sobered up and my mind cleared.

"You know I'm not good with all of the medical stuff, so I'll just let the doctor explain it all when he gets here."

He was trying to look at me, but he continued to avert his gaze if I asked about what was going on with me. Lucky for him, the doctor arrived just a couple of minutes later. He introduced himself to me, and pulled over a chair to the side of my bed.

"Mrs. Colley, my name is Dr. Nieves. I have been reviewing your labs and test results, and I'm afraid the news isn't as great as I'd like it to be." He paused, almost as if for dramatic effect, and then dropped the news that would forever change my life. "I'm very sorry, but you have stage four stomach cancer. There are treatments we can do, but they won't really add much more time. They are more about improving the quality of your life."

"What do you mean, add any more time? Am I dying?"

"Mrs. Colley, stage four is terminal. With the damage that I saw from the tests, I would estimate that you have approximately 4-6 months left to live with treatments."

"What? I'm going to die in the next few months? Are you serious?"

"There is a small percentage of people who make it a year, but I don't want to make you any promises."

This guy was unbelievable. He sat there and told me that I was going to die soon, and was worried about making me promises. I turned to Julian, who I hadn't realized had been holding my hand this entire time, and just stared at him in disbelief. He pressed his fingers against my palm and attempted a smile.

"Something must be wrong with those tests. I was just celebrating my birthday! I am not sick, there's no way. You need to fix that chart." I had turned back to face the doctor, and I was met with what seemed like cold, heartless eyes.

"Why don't I go over these test results with you? Perhaps if you saw the information yourself..."

"Dr. Nieves, can we have a moment, please? I think Elly might need some time to process", Julian said as he cut the doctor off midsentence.

The doctor left the room, stating that he would come back in a little while to start discussing treatment options. I was so confused, and just wanted to be back home in my own bed. Julian wasn't sure when we would get to leave, but he didn't seem very enthusiastic about the possibility that it would be that day.

It turns out that I wouldn't be able to leave for another 3 days. Within hours, I had an entire team of doctors assigned to me. By the time I was finally discharged, my calendar was filled with upcoming appointments and new contacts that I would be spending way too much time with. My whole world had come crashing down around me, and I didn't have any way to stop it from happening.

***

Five months had passed since that day, and I was still hanging in there. While the doctors had originally joked about me being sick to try to lose weight, getting down to a small size was the only bright side to all of this. I had learned to be proud of my bald head, even though there were days when I still felt the need to put on my wig, or at the least, a pretty scarf. They had me start the chemical infusions right away, but I never got used to them or the way they made me feel. Through it all, Julian stayed by my side, never once faltering in his abilities to be the world's best husband.

Another round of infusions were completed, so we checked out and started walking to the car. My pace had slowed down a bit lately, and I wondered if Julian had noticed it. If he had, he never bothered to mention it. He opened my car door for me, climbed in himself, and started the car. He handed me my squeeze pack of applesauce, a little tradition we had started as a way to help settle my stomach after each weekly infusion. Sucking the sweet concoction out of the packet reminded me of being a kid, and made me long for the earlier parts of my life, when things were so much easier and death wasn't constantly hovering over me. We rode home in silence, as the drugs tended to give me a headache.

When we pulled up to the house, Julian helped me inside to the bedroom. Infusions always equaled afternoon naps, and I was ready to get that one started. I crawled under the top sheet and promptly fell asleep. When I woke up, I could smell eggs wafting from the kitchen. I used to love cooking, but I hadn't had the energy to do it lately. Julian was never a great cook, but he was learning how to make some meals that wouldn't hurt my stomach, yet still had some flavor to them. That evening's cuisine would be poached eggs with toast, a common staple around our home. It wasn't a large meal, but I knew that I would get to enjoy a milkshake for dessert afterwards. My body was burning up so many calories trying to fight the cancer, I had to supplement with calorie-dense foods to keep it going. I would have loved a good burger and fries, but I couldn't handle the grease.

We ate our five star meal in the living room, planted in front of the television as we caught up on the last few episodes we had missed of our favorite show. When we were done, Julian grabbed both of our dishes and proceeded to clean everything up from dinner. After a while, I could no longer fight the fact that my energy was depleted, so I laid my head on his lap and stretched out on the couch. It was times like these that I was glad we had gotten one of those extra-large wrap around couches. There was plenty of room to sprawl out without cramping up the other person. Soon after getting comfortable, I fell asleep.

When I woke up, I realized that Julian had scooted over a bit and was now fervently typing away at his laptop. Still in a bit of a haze, I asked him what he was doing.

"Huh? Oh, I'm just looking something up. While you were sleeping, there was a breaking news story. I'm trying to see if I can find out more information on it."

"Breaking news? What happened?"

"Apparently someone who goes by the name Hacker has broken into the overseer's mainframe. They got a copy of the death dates for everyone, and now they're offering them for sale."

"Are you kidding me?" I sat up as I tried to imagine what exactly Julian was talking about.

"No, I'm serious. It's a huge story, and everyone is freaking out. They're trying to figure out who this person is and they're offering a hefty reward for any information that leads to their capture."

"So you're trying to figure out who they are?" I was so confused.

"I wish. We could certainly use that reward money. I'm just looking up stories right now to see what kinds of things have been put out there so far." He seemed deeply involved in his search.

"Have you discovered anything of value? What would you plan on doing if you found out something?"

"I don't know, I'm just curious. It would be pretty cool to know what dates our microchips are programmed to, don't you think?"

"I'm not really worried about what mine says. I can only beat the odds for so long, so I don't think the date on my chip will even matter." When I was given my diagnosis, I was told my life wouldn't last much longer. Did it really matter what date the overseers had given me? At the most, I probably had a few more months. Of course, it was a completely different scenario when it came to Julian. "If you could find out yours, would you do it?"

"With an asking price of $50,000, we could never afford it."

"I wasn't asking if we could afford it, I asked if you would do it." Julian took a minute to think about it. He was sticking his tongue out ever so slightly between his lips, a sign he was really concentrating on the matter.

"If we suddenly, magically came into $50,000, then sure, I wouldn't mind knowing. Since I don't see any fairies waving their wands around me, I'm not going to get my hopes up." He smiled, then closed his laptop and put it next to him. "It's a moot point, so let's not worry about it anymore. You passed out before we finished getting caught up on our show. Do you want to watch any more of it?"

"Sure, I'll try and stay awake this time", I said while giving him a little smirk. Nestling up next to his warm body, I managed to fight off the fatigue I was feeling long enough to complete watching the show. Without even realizing it, several hours had passed, and it was time to head to bed for the night. The clock chimed, signaling that it was eleven o'clock already. I knew that Julian had a lot of painting to do tomorrow, and he had to try to fit it in around working his shift at the restaurant. I no longer had the energy to sculpt any big projects, so all of our income now came from him. Occasionally I would be able to make some small trinket, and I might make a few dollars from it, but that wasn't steady money and we had bills to pay. Wishing we had more hours left in the day, we headed to bed.

I felt horrible that Julian had to do so much to take care of me. He didn't really get to enjoy the things that a man his age should be enjoying. We tried to have fun, but I was always so worn out, it made it difficult to really get into the moment. Most of the time, we would have friends come over to the house and hang out with us there. That way, if I got too tired to participate, I could just excuse myself and go lie down. Sadly, that happened more times than I cared to remember.

***

The next morning, Julian got up early and started on his latest piece. I awoke just as he was getting changed to go to the restaurant.

"Good morning, sleepy head. How are you feeling today?" There was nothing better than waking up to his smile.

"Doing okay. You about to head out?" I watched as he put on the tacky outfit that he was required to wear. Khaki pants were definitely not a good look on him.

"Yeah, pulling a full eight hour shift today. Do you need anything before I go?" He was always thinking about my needs before his, always putting me first.

"No, I should be good to go. Thanks, though."

"Okay then, I've got to get a move on. If you need anything, you know to just call work and they will get a hold of me." He hated not being able to have his cell phone at his side in case of emergency, but company policy said he had to lock it up during his shift.

"I know. Don't be late. I'll see you tonight. Love you."

"Love you, too." He gave me a quick kiss and headed towards the door. I could see him as he lingered before walking out, looking back at me. He always struggled with leaving me alone, constantly fearing the worst.

My energy level was usually at its highest first thing in the morning, so I took advantage of that and got showered and dressed. I ate a small breakfast, and then got comfortable on the couch with my laptop. I remembered the conversation I had with Julian last night about something having to do with the death dates and someone called the Hacker. I started doing searches to see what I could find out. It didn't take long, as the news seemed to be everywhere.

I was amazed at what I was reading. Anyone could find out what their death dates were now, as long as they could pay the steep price tag. I knew that Julian wanted to know, but he had it set in his mind that we could never afford it, so it didn't matter. He was right; we didn't have an extra $50, let alone

$50,000. Still, I really wanted to find a way to get that information for him. I looked through our monthly budget to see if there was anything we could cut back on to save some money.

We were not big spenders, so the charges that we had each month were mostly for necessary items. Of course, we did splurge on the occasional meal out or day trip somewhere if I was up to it. Nevertheless, the biggest expense was one that smacked me across the face almost every day. My infusions cost an outrageous amount of money, and that came out of our account each week.

I knew that if I talked to Julian about it, he would never agree with me. Those infusions were helping to keep me alive, but we both knew they wouldn't be able to work forever. I had already made it longer than the doctors had expected, and every day was like a bonus at this point. My energy had been waning, and I had already accepted my fate. On some days, Julian seemed to understand that our time together was limited, but on others, he acted like nothing was wrong and we would be enjoying our golden years alongside each other. I knew it was hard on him, and I wanted nothing more than to make sure he was happy. For all that he did for me, he deserved nothing less.

Without my infusions, we would have almost enough to pay the fee to the Hacker. To make up the difference, I could sell a few bigger pieces of my work. It would take a lot out of me to create them, but I had already received requests from people that I had initially rejected. I figured that if I could get them to commission those sculptures, I could put the money together with what we would save and surprise Julian. There were also some other ones I had already made taking up space in our house that could be sold. I thought it was a great plan, but I had to ascertain how I was going to pull it off.

The hardest part would be keeping it from Julian, as we never kept secrets from each other. One more infusion was scheduled for the next day, and then I could put my plan in place. I felt badly about hiding this from him, but I saw it as a gift I was giving him, and it just happened to be a surprise. I wasn't going to cut my life short; I was going to going to make his longer.

Chapter Nine

Asher & Silas

Encased in my cocoon of blankets, I stared at the multitudes of gift baskets that were sitting on my dining room table. I reached out to grab a tissue, making it just in time to catch the onslaught of sneezes that escaped my red and dry nose. This was supposed to be the best night of my life, but I was stuck at home, practically conjoined with the couch as I laid there, trying to get over the sickness that was controlling my body. I focused on staying awake long enough to hear if my name was called, fighting against the medicine I took earlier that evening. I felt my eyelids drawing down towards my cheeks, but I managed to push through just as I heard it.

"And the winner for best director is...Asher Stonefield!" I grabbed onto the arm of the couch through the fortress of comfort, stopping short of falling off and hitting the ground as I took in what was just said. I couldn't believe it! I felt that I deserved to win, that my work on *Forgotten Promises* was award worthy, but I wasn't going to get my hopes up after not even being nominated on the last three pieces that I put out. That was my moment, and I was able to experience it surrounded by items that loved ones had sent me, but not the people themselves. Most of the cast and crew were attending the awards ceremony, as many of them were nominated in their own categories. Those who weren't there were probably out celebrating with their own circle of special people. Perhaps a few of them had stayed home, simply enjoying the moment with their particular someone.

I didn't have a choice, as those nasty germs kept me stuck at home and away from all of the fun. While I felt like I might have been on the upswing, I didn't want to risk getting anyone else sick. Of course, the moment the announcement was made, my phone started blowing up. Everyone wanted to congratulate me and offer me words of encouragement and support. Between the lovely treasures that filled my home, to the many voices that filled my ear, I should have felt like the most loved person in the universe. I should have, but I most certainly did not.

As I said my goodbyes to those kind enough to reach out to me, I silenced my phone and allowed the drowsiness I had been wrestling with to take over. Drifting into a gentle sleep, I couldn't help but think about the one person I didn't hear from that night. Beckett did not reach out to me, and it made the feelings I was just starting to put in the past come crashing back like a wave against a wall. We had been together for nine years when he walked away from it all, just as I was wrapping up filming on this project.

***

"Where are you going? Put those bags away. Come on, Beckett, let's talk about this!"

"I need a change, Asher. I feel like things have gotten stagnant with us. You are always so busy filming all day, when you come home, all you want to do is sit around the house. Life is meant to be lived, and I want to experience all the things that it has to offer. If you must know, I'll be staying with Lucinda until I can get a place of my own."

"Lucinda? Really?" That bitch never liked me, so I'm sure she was as happy as a pig in slop to take Beckett in. She would probably try to use the time together to convince him he wasn't gay and that he should be with her. "Look, if it's excitement you want, let's take a trip somewhere. You name it. I am sorry you feel like things are so boring here, but I'm just really tired after being on set. I'll try harder; I'll make more time for you, for us."

"This isn't the first time we've had this conversation, and you know it. Every time you're working on a new movie, you are gone for long periods. When you're not actually filming, you're either in meetings planning the next job you are going to do, or lost with your head in some script. You have always put your job first, and I'm sick of it! To be honest, I think you were done with this relationship long before I was. You just didn't have the balls to actually end it."

"If I was done with it, why would I stand here and fight with you to stay? I love you, Asher, and I want to make this right. Tell me what you need from me so I can give it to you. Just please, don't go."

I was practically begging him to stay, trying to find a way to convince him that it was the right thing. Looking back, I didn't know if I was fighting for our relationship because I wanted him, or if I just didn't want to be alone. It didn't matter, though, as just moments after that, he opened the front door and left. That was over a year ago, but reliving it in my dreams made it feel like it just happened all over again.

***

I woke up from my narcotic fueled sleep still on the couch, but the blankets were strewn on the floor below me. I must have tossed them off during the night as my fever crept back up and my body overheated. The sun was streaming through the cracks where the curtains parted. My fever had broken and I was feeling much better, so I decided that maybe a shower would motivate me to start the day.

The cool water was refreshing against my skin, washing away the sweat and grime from the last few days. As I closed my eyes and let the drops race down my body, I suddenly remembered last night's announcement. Best director, Asher Stonefield. The speaker's voice echoed through my head repeatedly. Was I imagining it, brought on by the sickness or the medicine that had been coursing through my body? I stepped out of the shower, dried off, and grabbed my phone. There was a litany of messages waiting to be seen and heard, all congratulating me on my win. That solidified it, making the wondrous news of last night a reality.

I had all of the motivation I needed to get moving. After getting dressed, I started going through all of the celebratory remarks I had received, and began reaching out to those who were kind enough to contact me. After sending out a few responses, my phone rang in the midst of typing up a message.

"Hey Asher, it's Silas. How ya feeling, Mr. Best Director?"

"You know what they say; it's just nice to be nominated." I could hear Silas chuckling on the other end. "It feels freaking AMAZING! I just wish I could have been there to celebrate with everyone last night. Being sick sucks."

"If you're up for it, you're invited to come and join me for some brunch. I need some greasy stuff to get rid of this hangover. I'll fill you in on all of the details from the ceremony and the after parties. There was some crazy shit going on, man. You'll never guess who hooked up after a few too many drinks."

"Yeah, sure, I'll be there. Bucket Bites, as usual? I'll do my best not to cough on you."

"Gee, thanks, 'preciate it. Yeah, nothing like starting the day with some tiny buckets of food! Let's call it in 30, does that work for you?"

"I can do that. See you in half an hour!" I hung up the phone and looked in the mirror. I still looked somewhat sickly, but at least there was some color in my cheeks. Grabbing the blankets off the floor, I did a quick straightening up before heading out the door.

I could always count on Silas to have the day's gossip hot and ready for me. At just twenty-six, he was one of the younger crewmembers, and hadn't had enough time in the field to be jaded yet. I appreciated his friendship, and consistently had a good time when we hung out together. There were times being with him made me really feel all forty-five of my years, but most of the time he helped me to forget my troubles and just have a good time. He didn't see our age difference as an issue, and I tried not to let it drag me down.

***

The conversation was flowing freely as we talked about all of the work we had put into the movie over the last two years. From the multiple weeks of shooting, to waiting for all of the post-production work to be done. The time spent marketing it, and showcasing it at several film festivals before it was finally released into the arms of the awaiting public. Now was the time to enjoy the fruits of our labor. From what he was telling me about last night's celebrations, everyone was seemingly doing just that.

"It kills me that I missed out on everything. *Forgotten Promises* was my baby, and it's like I wasn't there for her first birthday. Now all of the stories and pictures won't have me in them."

"Well here, we can fix that!" Silas grabbed his phone, and practically jumped around to my side of the table. Holding it up above us at the perfect selfie angle, he leaned in and kissed me as I heard the distinct sound of the camera clicking our picture. "Now you're in a picture, and once I share it with everyone, you'll definitely be in a story!"

My mouth sat there agape as I tried to process what had just happened. I looked to Silas for direction, as I suddenly felt very lost. He returned to his seat, and started to pick at the crumbs that were left on his plate after he had devoured his food.

"So what's next, Mr. Director?" he asked me as he took a sip from what little remained in his glass. I just stared at his beautiful face, not sure exactly where he was going with that question. Thankfully, he didn't seem to notice my awkwardness. "Do you have another project in mind yet? I know of a certain out-of-work crew member that would just love to team up with you again." He smiled at me, and I could feel my heart settle back into my chest.

"I don't have any prospects right now, but I'm hoping that something good will come my way soon." Even though I had faith that *Forgotten Promises* would be a hit, it seemed that not many other people did. I hadn't been receiving many scripts lately, and I was getting worried that I wouldn't have another project to start on.

"Well, now that you're the king, I'm sure the scripts will come rolling in. Your majesty." He swept his arm across his chest and leaned forward, slamming his elbow into the table as he feigned a royal bow to me.

"Oh no!" I started to giggle, but then felt badly for doing so. I could see he was stifling his own snicker. "Very funny, but flattery will get you everywhere." I winked at him, and we both laughed, perhaps a little bit too loudly as we noticed people starting to turn our way.

We finished our meal, and he grabbed the tab, insisting it was his way of saying thank you for having him as part of my crew. I cracked some bad joke about how if I had known he would be paying; I would have waited to meet up for a nice dinner. Our laughter continued as we walked out the door and over to the lot where we were parked. We hugged goodbye, and I could have sworn I felt his arms linger just a little bit longer than usual around my back. Getting in my car, I waved farewell as I pulled away and headed home.

***

I attempted to clean up the house a bit, as it had gotten somewhat nasty while I was dealing with the first few days of being sick. I disinfected all of the surfaces and started up some laundry before needing to call it quits and head back to bed. I felt like I had just fallen asleep when I heard several pings in a row coming from my nightstand. I was so tired; I reached over and turned my phone off so as not to be disturbed. I had no idea what was happening while I slept, but I would find out upon waking up just two hours later.

129

When did THIS happen?

You + Silas = WTF?!

#MayDecemberRomance

My social media presence was suddenly overwhelmed with people questioning my life. Apparently, Silas had shared the picture he took of us, and everyone wanted to know what the meaning behind it was. My phone was once again overloaded with messages, but now they weren't all so congratulatory. Some people did not like the idea that we could be together. Others just wanted the particulars. Seeing as to how I didn't really know what was going on myself, I wasn't sure how to answer them. As I scrolled through my texts, I saw one from Silas.

I told you your name would be in a story.

He was right, but that story was still missing all of the details. I wanted to know what made him take that picture. Why did he kiss me? I mean, I've given my friends kisses on the lips before, but they lasted only a second long, and it was usually done when greeting or saying goodbye to someone. The kiss Silas planted on me? That one was definitely a good three seconds, and came out of nowhere. The lack of understanding was killing me, so I finally gave in and called him. Wouldn't you know it? Voicemail. I did my best to sound casual, and asked him to give me a shout when he got the chance.

I spent the next thirty-seven minutes pacing around my house, attempting to keep myself busy while I waited to hear from him. The messages and posts were piling up, but I didn't want to speak with anyone before I had a chance to discuss this with Silas first. As I picked up the phone, I could feel my heart racing in my chest. "Hello?"

"Hey Asher, I got your message. What's up?"

"Oh nothing, just wanting to thank my photographer for making my big win last night become the second most talked about story in my life today." I was hoping he could hear the smile in my voice.

"Oh, are people still talking about our picture? Geez, I would have thought something else would have caught their eye by now." There was definite sarcasm in his tone, but I still was not getting any hint of how he truly felt, or why he kissed me.

"I know, I would have thought we'd be old news by now." I let out a little chuckle, but even I could tell it sounded forced. "You know, everyone's asking me what our *deal* is."

"Nosy little fuckers. What did you tell them?"

"I haven't responded to anyone yet."

"Oh, okay."

There was something in his voice that almost sounded like disappointment. Was he expecting me to give a particular response? What did he think I was going to say? I felt like it was time to get some clarification. I didn't want to upset him, and I couldn't just ignore the situation. "To be honest, I really don't know what to tell them. I certainly don't want to speak on your behalf, and I'm not sure what's going on myself." There was a pause in the conversation, something that usually didn't happen when Silas and I were talking,

"I'm sorry to have put you in an awkward spot. It was a spur of the moment thing, I hadn't really thought about it. I almost didn't share it, but since I had already mentioned it to you that I was going to, I went ahead and sent it out. I guess I didn't really think about the consequences of my actions."

"You don't have to apologize. Isn't the saying, there is no such thing as bad publicity? Besides, I always enjoy a good kiss. I mean, picture." Oh no! No, no, no, no, NO!! Why must my mouth move faster than my brain?

"Oh really? Hmmm…." Silas got very quiet, and I felt like I was about to explode while waiting for him to speak again. His voice was soft, almost to the point of a whisper. "I enjoyed it, too."

My heart suddenly took residence in my throat, and each beat felt like a spasm against my tonsils. I tried to speak, but the words just wouldn't form together from the sounds that were slowly leaking out of my mouth. I hadn't had feelings like this for anyone since Beckett, and they took me completely by surprise. I knew that physically I desired Silas. After all, he was a bit of a gym fanatic with abs that you could trace through his shirt. We always enjoyed our time together, no matter what we ended up doing. The only thing that concerned me was our glaring age difference. Did it bother me because I didn't like it, or was it that I was more concerned with how others would see us? My mind was reeling, and I hadn't realized how quiet I must have gotten until I heard a small cough on the other end of the line.

"Asher? Are you still there?" he whispered so faintly.

He sounded a million miles away, and I realized that I wanted him closer.

"Yeah. I'm here. I wish you were here, too." Again, my mouth betrayed my brain. It felt as if my heart was slamming the door open, loudly announcing itself to the world. Sometimes I really hated being so emotionally available.

"I wouldn't exactly mind being there. I can come on over if you would like me, too. I don't want to impose."

The house still needed a major cleaning, but I was willing to risk being seen as a slob if it meant I could have Silas beside me.

"Having you visit is never an imposition. You'll have to excuse the mess, as the place is not currently up to my standards. Being sick really knocked me off my cleaning schedule."

"I'm not coming over to see the house, so don't even worry about it. Besides, I'm sure your idea of a messy house is probably closer to my idea of a clean one." He laughed in a way that made me feel more at ease about how messy my house really was. "I'll head out in a couple. I should be there in about 20-30 minutes."

We said our goodbyes, and I immediately started racing around like a chicken with its head cut off, putting away anything that was obviously out of place. I washed off the dishes that were in the sink, and made my bed. The laundry had finished, but I didn't have time to put everything away, so I left it in the machine for the time being. This was not the first time that Silas would be in my home, but it might just be the first time that being there *mattered*. Nothing would be perfect, but everything would be as close to it as I could make possible in the little bit of time that I had.

I was just tossing the last few knick-knacks into a basket by the fireplace when I heard the doorbell ring. I looked over at my security panel, even though I already knew it was him. He looked so good just standing there, and it made me smile to see him shuffling back and forth a bit while waiting to be let in. He looked like a nervous student outside of the principal's office, waiting on his fate. I opened the door and welcomed him inside.

"Just as I suspected, this is so the opposite of messy. I'll have to hire an entire cleaning crew to take care of my place before you see it for the first time."

The first time. I never really thought about how I hadn't been to Silas' home before.

Now I wasn't sure if I should be upset about that, or happy that his wording implied that I would be there more than once in the future. I decided to focus on the latter, and invited him to come and sit down in the living room. He took a seat on the sofa, and I wasn't sure if I should join him there, or sit across from him in one of the chairs. The chairs seemed a safer bet, so I headed over to one.

"Can I get you anything to drink? Wine, beer, soda?"

"No thanks, I'm good."

"Are you sure? Not even a water?" I was so nervous, I was looking for anything that would provide me with an excuse to stall the inevitable conversation we were about to have.

"I'm fine, really. Sit down. It makes me nervous when people stand around me while I'm seated."

I made my way to the chair and settled down into it. Crossing and uncrossing my legs several times, I tried to appear more casual than I was feeling. Really, I was just freaking out inside, and I couldn't get comfortable.

"It's really nice being here. I have wanted to talk to you, but I kept putting it off. I don't know why, really. I guess I just found excuses that didn't need to be found. I wasn't sure exactly where to start, or where it might lead, so I figured it would be easier if I didn't even try to begin anything. I mean, I know how great our friendship is, and I didn't want to risk ruining that we weren't on the same wavelength or something. Then there's what other people might say. It's just....am I making any sense?" He was rambling away, and I was doing my best to follow him. If I was reading him correctly, which I hoped I was, then he was making perfect sense, because I felt the same way.

"Silas, I could be taking this the wrong way and coming from completely out of left field, but I'm going to take a shot at it anyway. So, here goes.....I like you, and I think you like me, too. Not just as friends, but as something more. If we were in middle school, I would say that I "like *like*" you. It sounds like we both have the same fears and concerns, and we've both been too stupid to just come right on out and say something to the other. How am I doing so far?"

"I would say you weren't in left field, you were hitting it out of the ballpark. Moreover, that is the last sports reference you'll hear from this guy. I have wanted to ask you out for several months now. My nerves got the better of me repeatedly. I kept waiting for the perfect moment, knowing that no such thing truly exists. When I went to take our picture, I didn't really plan to kiss you. It just kind of happened. I was going to plant one on your cheek, but you could say I was pleasantly distracted. I knew that if I posted that picture, everyone would start talking. I figured that putting it out there sort of allowed me to let social media take away my nerves and just go for it. I was so worried that you might not feel the same way, and then I would have to try and fix everything."

"You have nothing to worry about fixing. Nothing is broken." I got up from my chair and joined him on the couch. It almost felt like some cheesy holiday movie scene, but I couldn't stop from seeing it through. I sat right next to him, our thighs touching ever so slightly. I touched his cheek, and his hand reached for mine. He leaned in and kissed me, even softer than the first time, if that was possible. I allowed my lips to linger on his a bit, not wanting the moment to end.

***

I heard the chime of my notifications go off in the other room, signaling a news update. Nothing was going to ruin this, so I ignored it for the time being. Nothing the overseers had to say was as important as the news that was being made at the moment. I could only hope that history was being made on my couch as the start of something new and wonderful, and not the beginnings of a very big mistake. Then another chime went off, and other sounds were heard coming from both Silas' and my phones. Obviously, something was going on that we needed to know about, so as much as we didn't want to stop, we grabbed our phones to see what the big deal was.

HACKER BREAKS INTO SYSTEM. DEATH DATES BEING HELD FOR RANSOM.

Silas and I looked at each other in disbelief, and then we both started laughing. It didn't really make sense that someone could hold a day of the year for ransom. The words were so big and flashy, but it was hard to take something like that seriously. I pictured a little calendar being restrained by someone at knifepoint, and it made me laugh even harder. Having a death date was just something we had accepted as part of our lives. I remember when I had the chip put in, and the experience was not a pleasant one. However, it seemed like forever ago at this point, and not something I thought about on a daily basis. Silas was a lot younger when he had his done, and the trauma of it all seems to have caused him to block out the memory of it. It wasn't really anything we had talked about together before, so this would be a new topic of conversation that we couldn't avoid approaching.

We sat there in silence as I turned on the television to see the breaking news reports on the main channel. It was all that was being talked about. This Hacker person had somehow gotten a hold of all of the death dates for everyone, and now you could find yours (or anyone else's) out for a fee. Whereas I felt like I was in a cheesy romance movie before, now I suddenly felt like we had changed channels to a science fiction one. The notification chimes kept coming in as more information was released about the situation. They didn't know who the Hacker was. They didn't know how they had managed to get through all of the security systems that were in place. They didn't know why the Hacker was doing this. All they could seem to figure out was that it probably had to do with money, since the person was asking for an awful lot of it if you wanted to get your death date.

The overseers were asking for anyone with any information to please come forward. They promised rewards for those who did, and consequences for those who would be found withholding information. You could feel the tension that was taking over the room, but when I looked down, I could see that Silas was holding my hand. The stress of the news that was blaring at us was slowly starting to melt away as I let the warmth of his palm against mine expand to my fingertips.

"This is so weird. Why would someone want to know everyone's death dates? What do you think they plan to do with the information? I mean, obviously they want money, but how many people do you really think have access to that much just laying around as petty cash?" Silas did not come from money, and he worked hard to earn every penny that he had. I wasn't sure if he was asking because he was just curious, or if he was thinking about how he would never be able to afford to pay if he wanted to find out.

"I don't imagine there are a lot of people out there like that. Even so, how many people would really want to find out? Can you imagine knowing the day that you were supposed to die? If money weren't an issue, would you want to know yours?"

"I don't know. I mean, there are so many ways it can affect the way you would live if you knew. I wouldn't want to miss any opportunities if I knew my life might be cut short. Then I have to think about what changes I might make, and how they would influence what might have been otherwise. You know?

Like, would I be altering my life for the better, or would it just appear that way, and the things I would miss out on wouldn't matter since I wouldn't know about them."

We talked more about it as we listened to what the reports were saying. Together we came up with tons of hypothetical questions, but we didn't have any answers. Any time I tried to nail down a concrete answer from Silas as to whether or not he would want to know his death date, he either avoided the question entirely, or simply stated that he wasn't sure. After a while, we got hungry and decided to order in some food.

The day's events were exhausting, and I was so thankful that I had Silas to share them with. The more I thought about him, the more I realized that I had fallen for that hottie hard. Every time I looked into his eyes, I imagined a life together. It was really weird. In the span of mere seconds over a friendly brunch, our relationship went from co-workers and friends, to the potential to become so much more. How had I not seen it before? When I took the time to think about it, I could look back and see that there were flirtations happening here and there. Jokes with an extra hint of innuendo were passed between us on set. The signs weren't blatantly obvious, but they were a little bit clearer now that there was some context attached to them.

After filling our bellies, we decided to watch a movie and just enjoy each other's company. There were a few kisses exchanged, but we mostly just snuggled up and watched in silence. I think we were both so worn out from trying to process everything; it was easier to just ignore it for now and deal with it later.

I really wanted to invite Silas to spend the night, but with things being so new, I wasn't sure it would be a good idea. He must have sensed it, too, as once the movie was over, he slowly sat up and started to get off the couch.

"I'd better get home. I don't know if Lancelot's feeder had anything left in it, and I don't want him to starve", he chuckled.

"Who's Lancelot?"

"He's the world's fattest kitty. He is a sweet cat that I found hiding near my place. He was sickly looking and didn't have any markers, so I took him in. Of course, I've spoiled him rotten since day one, so now he thinks he runs the place!"

Good looking, sweet, *and* he took in a stray kitty? Just another reason for me to fall for this guy.

"Yeah, I would hate to be the reason your baby went without a meal. I am really glad you came by and we got to talk. I would like to take you out on an official date. Let's give all of those naysayers something else to gossip about. What do you say?"

"Asher, I think that would be really nice. Are you free tomorrow night?"

"Yeah. How does 6:00 sound?"

"That works for me!"

"Okay, it's a date, then! I'll be picking you up, so just message me your address. Oh, and don't forget to call that cleaning crew to have them come by in the morning!" We both laughed, and gave each other a big bear hug.

As much as I didn't want to see him go, I was thrilled that we had plans already set up for the next night. I called one of the best steakhouses in town, and was lucky enough to grab a last minute reservation. I went to clear off the notifications from my phone, and couldn't help but replay my conversations and kisses from earlier in my head. I was still wondering why he wouldn't give me a straight answer when it came to finding out about his death date. The more I thought about it, the more I realized that it didn't just matter to me whether or not Silas wanted to know. When it came down to it, I was the one who wanted to know. After having Beckett walk out of my life so suddenly, I was scared that if things worked out with Silas, he might suddenly leave me, too. When we talked about the death dates being revealed, I told him that I was considering finding mine out. I felt that life was about to take a turn, and I didn't want to run the risk of it all ending and not being able to plan for it. I wanted to make sure that I would be around long enough to enjoy everything that might be coming to me. Winning the award came with it a sense that the tides were turning. Now not only would I get more chances to make another great film, but perhaps this was the moment when I would get another chance at love.

The moon was shining a brilliant light into my bedroom while I got changed and ready for some sweet dreams. I had made a decision, but I wasn't sure if I was ready to tell Silas about it yet. I was going to find out how to reach the Hacker and get my death date. I could hear Beckett's words echoing in my head. *Life is meant to be lived.* It had taken me a while to fully understand what that phrase really meant, but I finally got it. I wanted to live my life, and I wanted to have Silas by my side as I did. That was why I planned to find out his death date, too.

Chapter Ten

The Blank

The skies were a dark gray, and the smell of rain was in the air. The ground was thirsty, and the seeds hiding below would welcome the liquid refreshment. I was beginning to worry that my crops would not grow enough this year, leaving me with a lack of food necessary to survive. If the fruits and vegetables were lacking, I would also be limited in what I could feed the livestock. My little slice of paradise was run with order, and when things were not "just so", chaos could easily ensue. That day I saw that a change was coming, and it was one that would bring a smile to my face. I raised my hands to the sky, and thanked the space around me for providing me the means to live as I did. Just as I did this, the first droplets caressed my cheeks, and I opened my mouth to welcome their kindness.

Walking back to the house, I started to pick up my pace as the rain began to come down a little bit faster, quickly turning into a deluge. I was still about half a mile from the entrance, so my jog rapidly turned into a sprint.

Finally seeing the bright blue door in the distance, I broke out into a full run as the weight of my now soaked clothing tried to weigh me down. My fingers reached out for the silver handle, as I threw my weight behind me, pulling the heavy door open and flinging my body inside. There was an ambient chill, as the fire had started to die down in my absence. I quickly grabbed a couple of logs and manipulated the embers so that the new wood would quickly catch.

As I began my ascent up to my bedroom, Trevor shuffled up beside me, and drops of water fell from my pants onto his matted coat. He followed me upstairs, and laid down next to the bed as I started to undress and grab some dry clothing to put on.

"Hey Trev, how's it going buddy? Did you miss me? Be thankful you stayed inside today, that rain came out of nowhere! It's a good thing though, isn't it buddy? We definitely need it, as long as it comes down at a slow and steady pace so the grounds don't flood."

I gently patted him on the head, looking into his sweet eyes. The years had been kind to him, but there was a white film that had slowly started to creep over his eyes, threatening to take his vision. His hearing had been declining gradually, and his energy was definitely not what it used to be. I didn't have an exact age for him, but I placed him at around 12 years based on our time together. Trevor was a special friend, and I would miss him when his time came to an end. Thankfully, dogs weren't given that nasty chip, so he could live out his life as long as possible with me.

***

It was ten years ago that I first found Trevor, or should I say that he found me. I was working on the farm, feeding some cattle, when he came lumbering up the land. My sense of shock was unimaginable, as I do not have any neighbors for about 100 miles surrounding me. This poor dog was severely malnourished and dehydrated, and was covered in such filth; I didn't know what color his fur was until he had been through several washings. As pleased as I was to see this

151

creature before me, I felt an immediate sense of dread, as I wondered where his human was. I looked around briefly, but my first priority had to be the ball of grime and muck before me.

The dog seemed to be friendly, and was happy to follow me back to the barn. I grabbed an apple from the barrel, and reached into my pants to grab my knife and slice off a piece for the pup. Crouching down low, I held the chunk of freshness between my thumb and pointer, extending my hand out towards him. Slowly, and with caution, he inched his way towards me, sniffing the air as he approached the shiny treat. When he got close enough, he opened his mouth and snatched the apple from my hand. He chomped away at it, and looked longingly at me for more. I was happy to oblige, and cut another slice for him. He quickly took it once again, and waited for more. As I could tell it had been a while since he ate, I didn't want to give him too much and make him sick. I got up and went to get the hose, hoping he wouldn't freak out. I turned the water on very low; letting him see the first few drops trickle out. He came up to drink from it, and I didn't stop him. While he drank, I let some of the water collect in my hand, and I carefully rubbed it against his fur. He would occasionally pause and look up at me to see what I was doing, but never tried to stop me. I placed the hose onto the ground and went to increase the water flow a little bit more. I watched him from a distance, keeping an eye to make sure he accepted the change. Once I felt it was okay to do so, I walked back over to him and began to raise the hose towards his back. My worries about him getting antsy were quickly assuaged as he stood there calmly and let me rinse the mess off his fur. There was so much dirt; it was not an easy task. Every so often, he would raise his head and try to drink the water coming from the hose. My hands were soon covered in mud, grass, and who knows what else that started to melt off this poor beast.

After several rounds of cleansing, I felt that I had gotten him the best he was going to get. I grabbed a towel from a nearby stall and rubbed him down. He shook himself dry several times, seemingly happy with his new appearance. He was extremely thin and frail looking, but he had an energy to him that showed he was younger than he appeared. I think he was just so happy to have a place to rest after what must have been quite a long journey from home. I needed to finish feeding the cattle that I was tending to when he first arrived, so I returned to my previous task, waiting to see what he would do. I was happy to see him follow me out to the field, perhaps a little unsure of his surroundings, but seemingly feeling secure by my side. He stayed with me as I did my rounds, and when I was through, he came back to the house with me to settle down for a meal. I mixed up some chicken and veggies for him, and set out a bowl of water to wash it down with. He was delighted to eat up the goodies, and almost appeared to have a smile on his face. I put down a pile of blankets on the floor in front of me, but this dog wanted nothing to do with them. Instead, he used what little energy he had left in him for the day, and he jumped up onto the couch to lay down next to me. Later that night, he joined me on my bed, becoming the first living being to share that sacred space with me. Even after all of that time, he still held that distinction.

***

The storm continued to drop down buckets outside as I went back downstairs and started to prepare some lunch. The hens have been giving me quite the bounty lately, so I was able to enjoy a large omelet with some potato hash. I scrambled up some extra eggs for Trevor, and then settled down to do some reading. The sound of the rain as it hit the roof was extremely calming, and I soon found myself getting sleepy. Grabbing the throw from the back of the couch, I placed my book on the table and snuggled underneath the comfy blanket. Trevor soon accompanied me at my feet, and together we drifted off to the soothing concert that nature provided us.

When I awoke, several hours had passed, and I knew that I wouldn't have much more daylight left to get my chores done. "Hey Trev, we practically slept the day away! I've gotta get a move on and get things done." I realized that the noise from outside had quieted down, and the rain had stopped. I folded up the blanket and placed it back over the couch. With the fresh rains, I thought about taking the boat out on the lake to get some fish, but decided there were more important things to be done first. Headed to the greenhouse, I left Trevor behind to continue napping on the couch. In the next week or so, I would need to start turning over my crops, preparing for the colder weather plants to go in. Over the years, I had learned to base my diet on what I was able to grow out here. Keeping the livestock in a steady breed, I never had to worry about a shortage of meat. My fruit trees and vegetable assortment helped to provide me with a steady balance of vitamins and minerals, aiding in maintaining my health and avoiding sickness. It was definitely a challenge the first few years, but I had learned to adjust to the rhythms of nature. It was a dance we did throughout the days, one that would train me in the ways of survival. I wasn't quite sure if I would make it in the beginning, having worked hard and fast to learn how to live off the grid. The way the world was crumbling, I fortunately had started learning about alternative ways to live as a precaution. Once the leaders started enforcing chipping, I rushed to gain the knowledge needed to make it on my own. I wasn't going to follow their rules, so I had to figure out how to live within my own.

***

As a young boy, I always had an interest in playing in the dirt and discovering how things grew and survived outside. My father passed away when I was only an infant, so my mother was happy to allow me to occupy myself. This provided her some much needed time to get things done, and gave me an education that came naturally, not just from within the confines of a classroom. I can recall holding onto squirming insects that tried desperately to get away from my intensely peering eyes. When I was about seven years old, I was gifted a microscope, which became to me what a favorite teddy bear or doll might have been to other children. I carried that thing around with me everywhere I could. It was nestled safely inside of a dark green box that had almost a scale like texture to it. Inside were foam cutouts that kept it from bouncing around, with slots for my slides. I would change out the slides every few days, always creating new ones from the things that I would find on my adventures. From pieces of leaves, to scraps of fabric, to the exoskeletons of bugs they had left behind, nothing was safe from the piece of glass with the little coverslip placed over it.

Seeing as how we didn't have a lot of money, my mother quickly learned how to make a little go a long way. I watched her as she sewed my clothes, repairing little tears here and there to try and make each piece last until I had outgrown it. She would purchase meat to be eaten only one or twice a week, preparing mostly plant based meals as they cost less to make. Most of our meals were made from scratch, and every leftover from one meal was eaten as another. Since it was just the two of us, we entertained each other, creating games using our imagination. Thanks to holidays and birthdays, we did have a television and gaming system, but I wasn't as interested in those as I was in exploring the world around me. I was lucky enough to get my own computer when I won it as a prize in a local contest, and that allowed me to research the things I was most curious about. Most of my time was spent with my nose in a book, though. I loved reading stories that allowed me to venture into worlds unknown, drifting off into the idea of who I could become. The history books really held my attention, too. With all of the things that went on around me, I found it fascinating to read about what life was like even just a few decades before I was born. The world was so different when my mother was growing up; I had a hard time believing that the books were actually non-fiction. I didn't know it then, but those books would soon be disappearing, making me appreciate what I had read even more.

Once I had finished my schooling, I knew that I wanted to pursue studies in agriculture. All of the time I spent outside only solidified my love for nature and the wonders it held. The plants and animals I had spent so much time learning about as a child continued to pose more questions in my mind as an adult. I registered for classes at the local university, and began my journey to gain as much knowledge as I could on the world around me. As I discovered more about nature, I realized how many uses the different parts of it held.

Stretching my knowledge, I read up on how to manipulate it. I studied skills such as glassmaking and forging.

Moving out on my own, I didn't get complete freedom. My living space was not large, and I shared it with two other people. The monthly payments weren't cheap, so I spent the time I wasn't studying working at a local furniture store where they handmade each piece. It was a small establishment, but the pay was good, and they trained me on how to make the pieces with them. I was amazed at the skill and precision they had as they carved out the wood and laid the fabric. On my one-year anniversary of working there, they gave me a beautiful chair as a gift to take home. It was on that chair that I was sitting when I first heard of the plans for the microchipping that would be taking place.

***

Living in Gamma, I could see how we didn't have enough space for everyone that resided there. With all of the destruction that had taken place over the last few years, each quadrant had limited areas that were sustainable enough for people to live in. Resources were sparse, and finding anything beyond what you were granted by the overseers was difficult, if not impossible. The weekly vouchers allowed you enough to survive, but that was about it.

There had been talk of how the overseers were working to fix the problems at hand. Teams of scientists were trying to come up with more viable ways of creating food sources in the harsh conditions we were experiencing. Plants were crossbred to try to find new and improved species that might thrive in the current environment. There were whispers of forced sterility to keep the numbers of people living there lower. Every day you would hear something new on how the world would be getting better, even if you didn't see it happening around you. Then the day came when the big announcement was made. We weren't told exactly what would be happening, but as I sat in my beautiful chair, I heard the announcement come over the airwaves.

"Citizens of the Gamma quadrant, please be sure to check your inboxes for a special message from your local overseer. You will each be assigned a number, along with an appointment date and time. When it is time for your appointment, please bring your letter with you to your designated area. There will be further instructions given to you at that time. These appointments are mandated by law, and if you do not attend yours, there will be legal and dire repercussions."

I looked at my roommate, who was sitting on the couch across from me. He looked just as confused as I did. "What the hell was that about?" I asked him as I got up to grab a snack.

"I don't know, man, but it sounds creepy. Why do you think they won't tell us what's going on?"

"No clue, but using terms like legal and dire repercussions means it can't be good." I rifled through the pantry looking for something salty to munch on, but nothing was there to satisfy my craving. "I'm gonna run to the store. Need anything?

"Depending on what that message was about, I might need something stiff for later. If you want to pick up a bottle of Blaze and something to mix it with, I'll pay you back when you get home."

"Sounds good. If you hear anything else while I'm gone, give me a shout and let me know. I just have a bad feeling about all of this, but I could be wrong. At least, I'm hoping I am." I grabbed my keys and walked out the door. My mind was reeling with possibilities of what the overseers could want. Requiring every citizen to attend some event, it had to be important. Nevertheless, why wouldn't they give us information on what it was? Why the big secret?

My roommates and I were all assigned different dates for our appointments. Antonio went first, just three days after the initial announcement was made. When he first came back into the house, there was something *off* about him. Physically, he appeared to be just fine, but the way he carried himself as he walked through the door was different. His head hanging low, his face expressionless, I was worried about him.

"Tone, what happened? What was the appointment all about?"

He raised his head just enough to look me square in the eyes and said, "They know when I'm going to die. They are going to kill me. They're going to kill us all."

Thinking they might have given him some weird drugs or something, I tried to figure out what he was talking about. "Uh, what do you mean they're going to kill us all? You high or something? What did they give you?"

"Dude, I'm not high. The only thing they gave me was this fucking microchip." He pointed to the back of his head, and I could see a tiny spot at the base of his hairline where it looked like he slipped the last time he cut his hair, and now there was a tiny patch missing. "I told you, they're going to kill me. And you. And everyone else in this world."

Okay, there was definitely something going on with Antonio, and I didn't think I was going to get a straight answer out of him at this point. He said he was going to lie down for a bit, so I just shrugged it off and figured I would find out what really happened once he sobered up or fixed whatever else was going on with him. A few hours later, he came out of his room and sat down in the chair next to the couch, where I was sitting and catching up on my studying.

"Feeling any better, man? Still think everyone is going to be killed?" I started laughing, realizing just how insane it sounded as the words came out of my mouth.

Antonio started rubbing the back of his neck, and I could see him wincing as something there was causing him pain. He turned towards me and smiled a wicked grin that turned up one side of his mouth ever so slightly. He then proceeded to tell me what happened at his appointment, and what instructions he, along with every other citizen that was there, were given. He explained the concept of death dates to me as tears started to roll down his face.

I wasn't quite sure what to make of all of it, as it sounded like something I might have read about in one of the classic science fiction books from my childhood. I remembered learning about mass executions and attempts at population control in my history classes, but those were done when someone tried to get rid of one type of group, not the entire world. I didn't want to believe him, but the details he had were so specific and clear, and then there was the issue of the scar on the back of his head. It wasn't until the next evening, when my other roommate came back from his appointment and told me the same thing, showing me the same scar that I knew it was truly happening. It was real, and my appointment was only five days away.

I didn't have much time, so I made a quick list of the things I would need to do. There was no way I was going to allow the overseers to slice me open and stick some technical device into my head. I was a firm believer in nature and all of its glory. When it was my time to die, then I truly believed that I didn't have a say in it, and neither did the overseers. Who were they to choose when my life would end? I was terrified, but I knew I had to stop this from happening to me. Of course, if

I attempted to just skip out on my appointment, I would be discovered, and as the announcement had clearly stated, the consequences would be *dire*.

My love of reading was about to pay off in a grand way. I knew of areas where no one lived, but where hopefully, life would be viable. I had the skills to create things with my hands, thanks to my training at my job. Watching my mom over the years when I was younger helped me understand how to live off barely anything when necessary. It was going to be a struggle; there was no doubt in my mind. If I could just get what I needed and get away, there was a chance I could make it. At this point, a chance was better than the alternative if I stayed there.

I gathered up some maps of the areas I would be traversing, and bought the supplies necessary to start things up. Seeds and starter plants were purchased to start crops, tools were carefully wrapped in protective blankets, and clothes were packed up in weatherproof containers. Of course, I couldn't leave my books behind, but I was limited in how many I could take. I tried to focus on ones that would make good resources, and not just be pure entertainment. With just a few days to get everything done, time was not on my side. Once I decided on my location, I loaded up my car and headed out. Thankfully, I had chosen the larger model SUV when purchasing my last car, so I had enough room for everything.

The hardest part was saying goodbye. I couldn't let anyone know where I was heading, but I didn't want to just disappear and have people worry about me. With both of my parents gone, and no real extended family to speak of, it was only my closest friends that I needed to tie things up with. I was never good at in person communication, so I decided to compose a letter instead. Without being able to give any details about my future, I just kept it brief, and made copies for each person. I added a few personal details to each one so it didn't appear to just be a form letter without any love behind it. For my roommates, I included my share of the monthly payment for the next month. I wasn't going to need money once I arrived at my new location, so I cleaned out my accounts to have money for travel and headed out.

***

The drive there would take me about thirty hours non-stop, so I decided I could split it up over three days. That would give me enough time to gather more supplies along the way if I needed them, and still get there before my appointment time would come up. I would be set up and starting my new life before anyone would have a chance to realize I wasn't going to be there. Food wasn't a problem, as I mostly ate at local restaurants along the way. I kept a cooler in the car for drinks and snacks, helping along the long stretches where I might not find a place to eat. For two of the nights I was able to get a hotel room to crash in and get some good sleep. On my last night, I was getting so far away from civilization; I had to sleep in my car. It wasn't as bad as I thought it would be, as I just laid out my sleeping bag across the seats I had folded down, and then snuggled up in my blankets. I awoke with the sunrise, and headed to my final destination.

I had heard of this area in passing previously. No one had mentioned the specific location, but talk was made about how it was never incorporated into the four quadrants. It had such natural beauty to it, but was too far away from other areas to be considered of any value. Once I found the largest open expanse, I turned off the road and continued driving for about an hour. That way I felt secure in my belief that no would easily be able to find me. It was a piece of land that didn't have much to it, but it was all that I needed. There were plenty of trees on the property, and a small lake nearby would provide a good starting water source. I had a lot to do, and there was no time to waste. Arriving early in the day allowed me plenty of daylight to start gathering materials. The first step was chopping down trees for firewood and building materials. The temperature was moderate during the day, and thankfully would not start getting too cold at night for a few months. The fire would mostly be used for cooking and water purification at this point. By the end of the day, I had managed to cut down five decently sized trees. As nightfall was approaching, I set up my tent and grabbed the solar lantern I had placed earlier so I could have a light source. While enjoying a meal of rehydrated beef stew, I took out my journal and started documenting the day's events. Today may not have had anything special happen, but it was the first day of my new life. On this day, I would become a solo frontiersman. A man technically on the run from the overseers. I didn't know if I would ever engage with civilization again, if there would ever be a time when I could safely return without threat of actions taken against me. All that mattered today was that I was free.

Time passed quickly, and I was able to build a nice home for myself. Using my knowledge of furniture building, I had created a decent set up with places to sit, eat, and a nice bed to sleep on. I had even created a little bookshelf to hold what was left of my personal library. I'll admit, it was lonely being out there all by myself, but when times got rough, I just kept reminding myself what was waiting for me if I returned to where I came from. I was able to get my crops to grow just as my food supply that I had brought with me was running out. I did find some fresh meat to hunt, and had started constructing corrals to keep the beasts in, hoping they would eventually breed. As the years went on, my house was expanded, a full barn was constructed for the animals (as they did indeed breed), and my journals filled up with details of my life, my hopes, and my dreams.

***

Standing in the greenhouse all of those years later, I could see just how far I had come. I was surrounded by life, and I got to live mine the way that I chose. As I started to cut some herbs from their pots, I saw Trevor slowly coming my way. Sometimes I thought he should have been named Shadow, as he loved to stay by my side. I grabbed a piece of lettuce and handed it down to him. He happily munched on it, and looked up to me for more.

"Not now, boy, we need to get everything picked and inventoried. Gotta make sure we have enough to last us in case today's rain was a fluke. When we get back inside I'll get you a treat, okay?"

Trevor looked up at me, seemingly understanding what I had said. He happily followed me around the greenhouse as I continued to pull and clip the plants that were ready to be taken and consumed. When our box was full, Trevor and I walked back to the house to empty it out. I organized our items, counting out each type of plant to see how much we had. I could see our numbers weren't as high as they should have been, but I hoped it would be enough to last us. I knew that the fields and the orchards were getting dry, so the greenhouse was something I really relied on to help keep afloat. As much as I enjoyed the beautiful sunshine that brightened each day lately, I longed for the rains to come and soak the parched earth.

As promised, I grabbed a treat for Trevor once all of the food was put in the kitchen. I reached into the basket and grabbed him a dehydrated pig's ear. He grabbed it, and settled down onto the couch to quietly chomp away at it. Having him in my life had truly been remarkable. There had been times when I wasn't so sure how I would get through to the next day. Times I wanted to just give up and

173

face whatever future laid before me back amongst the others in society. I had missed my friends, my co-workers, my schoolmates. Life would be so much easier to just return. Then I would look at Trevor, and how easy his life was with me. He wanted nothing but food in his belly, a warm blanket, and some love. I was inspired by the simplicity, and knew that it meant I could go on. Whenever I had doubts, I would remind myself of how Trevor found me, and how great our lives were together. He needed me, and that gave me a purpose. As long as he was by my side, I knew everything would be all right.

Chapter Eleven

The Stevensons

I barely had a chance to view her tiny form when the doctor rushed her onto a small table to the side of the delivery room. I wasn't even allowed to cut the cord, a moment I had been looking forward to as a first-time father. There were many murmurs amongst the staff, nurses speaking in hushed tones while rushing back and forth within the four walls. I just stood there, holding Emilie's hand while they cleaned her up. She was so tired, sweat dripping down her face, hair matted across her forehead, yet she never looked more beautiful. Our ear-to-ear smiles quickly faded as we watched the chaos unfold before us. We kept asking what was wrong, but no one would give us any answers. After a few minutes, but what seemed like an eternity, our bundle of joy was whisked away, out of what we thought was her safe, welcoming space.

"Gerald, what's going on? Where are they taking her?" Emilie asked me as she squeezed my hand.

"I don't know, honey, but I'll find out. Nurse? Excuse me, can you please tell me where they're taking our daughter to?"

The nurse explained to me that they were taking her to the Neonatal Intensive Care Unit, or NICU, and that the doctor would be in momentarily to give me the rest of the details. I looked over at Emilie, her body having been put through so much in the last few hours, and wondered what was running through her mind.

"It'll be okay. Dr. Pembroke will be right back, and we'll find out what happened." I leaned over Emilie and wrapped my arms over her sides. The nurse was just finishing up with her, and then she, too, would leave the room.

We were all alone, with nothing but the craziest of thoughts left to run through our minds. Believe me, when you are in that situation, your mind really does come up with the absolute worst-case scenarios. We just held each other, grasping for answers to questions we didn't even know how to ask. At some point, Dr. Pembroke returned to the room. We were so lost in our own heads; we didn't even realize she had come in. A gentle rap on the door broke the quiet in the room.

"Mr. and Mrs. Stevenson, I know you must be wondering what happened to your daughter. Rest assured she is in safe hands. Upon her delivery, we noticed something that did not show up in her ultrasound. It is a pretty telltale sign of hydranencephaly. I'm not sure how we missed it, but we have taken her up to the NICU to get a more thorough diagnosis and understanding of what we are dealing with."

"Wait, what are you talking about? How could you not see something with the multitude of ultrasounds Emilie had? How did you just *miss* something?" I was livid, absolutely livid. Over the course of the last nine months, Emilie had half a dozen scans done, and every single time they told us that our daughter looked great. Every. Single. Time.

"Mr. Stevenson, it seems that your daughter has an enlarged head, which suggests to us a diagnosis of hydranencephaly. As I stated previously, we are working to get a better understanding of what might be going on. I don't want to offer a permanent diagnosis

177

until I am absolutely sure. We will run some tests, get some bloodwork going, and I will be able to give you a better answer in a few hours. Until then, get some rest, and enjoy your time together. You know that a newborn brings with it many challenges, even without any medical complications. Get some food, take a nap, and I'll be back when I have more information to offer you."

With that, Dr. Pembroke turned around and left the room. We weren't given any time to ask questions of her, nor yell at her for not seeing the signs earlier in the pregnancy. We were just left there, two new, first-time parents, in shock and confusion. Emilie immediately started thinking of all of the things that she could have done while pregnant that could have caused this. Did she not get enough sleep? Did that occasional glass of wine that the doctor told her would actually be good for her turn out to be the problem? Was she too stressed, and passed all of that tension on to our then unborn child? If she could think of it, then it could have been the reason. She never sought any reasons to blame me, nor nature itself. If something was wrong with our daughter, then she had to have been the cause of it. My lovely Emilie, she takes on the pressures of the entire world on her tiny shoulders.

While trying to reassure her, I kept pushing away thoughts of things that I could have done, or what we could have encountered that might have brought this on. There had to be a reason, and we were going to figure it out. I grabbed my computer and started searching for information on hydranencephaly. My eyes glazed over as I sat next to Emilie, watching page after page of words, pictures, and graphs scroll across the screen. We were only scaring ourselves, causing greater misery than anyone else could bring to us. I was fixated, lost in the world of information that overwhelmed me. I kept pointing things out to Emilie, but after a while, I noticed her looking away.

"Gerald, we're just making this worse. Let's put the computer away and wait for Dr. Pembroke to come back. Remember, she said that it wasn't a definitive diagnosis yet. They have to see the test results. We are focusing on the disease, and not on our daughter. We brought a new life into the world today. Our daughter is here, and she doesn't even have a name yet."

Wow. Those words hit me like a slap across my face. I was so concerned with finding out about what might be *wrong* with our daughter; I forgot to take the time to think about all of the many things that were *right* with her. She was taken from us so quickly; we hadn't even had a chance to hold her yet. There she was, alone in a room with medical personnel running tests on her, and all we could think about was how to fix a problem we weren't even sure she had yet. The nametag on her bassinet would simply read "Baby Girl Stevenson". We needed to speak her name into existence, giving her life outside of this sterile environment.

"I know we had narrowed it down to three choices. Are you ready to make the final decision?" I wasn't sure which name to choose, so I was hoping that Emilie had made the decision on her own. When I pictured saying her name for the first time, it was while holding her gently in my arms, looking down at her as I rocked her to sleep. Now here we were, trying to choose a name so that our daughter was not just another statistic in the NICU.

"Personally, I think that with everything that's happening right now, we should go with Blythe. It just feels right."

She was right, that was the name our daughter needed to have. A name that meant happy or cheerful. Blythe. A name that was as beautiful as our daughter was. I looked at Emilie's face, and for the first time since Blythe was taken out of the room, I saw her smile. I wanted to freeze time, to stay in this moment as long as I could, knowing what was waiting for us as the minutes ticked by. This was the feeling that I wanted to experience on this special day. Not the anxiety, not the worry, not the fear. I wanted this feeling of complete and utter joy to take over my body. Looking at my wife, and seeing her smile, that was everything to me. Unfortunately, time did not freeze, and it was mere moments later when Dr. Pembroke came into the room.

"We ran some tests, and I'm sorry, but my suspicions were correct." Dr. Pembroke was looking directly at Emilie as she pronounced the words that would forever change our lives. I could see the sadness in her face. She was trying to maintain her professionalism, but her eyes were filling with tears. "I've put together some information on hydranencephaly for you to look over, and I'm here to answer any questions you might have." Dr. Pembroke handed me a folder and started explaining to us what this diagnosis meant. Blythe had a rare birth defect that effects brain development. She was missing the right and left hemispheres of her cerebrum. Where they were supposed to be, she had cerebrospinal fluid filling in the space. Her life expectancy wasn't supposed to be long, and for the time that she was supposed to live, she might suffer from seizures, vision problems, breathing, and digestion problems. She would be given a shunt inside her skull to help drain the fluid, and would need medications for the other issues later in life if she survived. Everything that was said seemed so negative. Emilie and I just listened, not sure of how to react. We were being told our baby girl might not make it through the night, and if she did, to not expect her to live much longer. I remembered reading a few blog posts from people whose children had this disease while I was frantically searching through my computer earlier, and were still alive as they entered double digits. It might have been rare, but it was still a possibility. I was grasping for promises unseen, and I was going to hold on tight.

I turned to Emilie, watching as tears streamed down her face. This was not what we had expected. She was so stoic, refusing to give in to the pain she must have been feeling inside. I was still in shock, but I was slowly coming to terms with our situation. We took turns asking questions about treatments, medications, and how to handle everything once we got home. After all was said and done, our focus was on the fact that we still had a new little person to take home and start a life with.

"Dr. Pembroke, when can we see Blythe?" It was the first time Emilie had said her name to someone else, and it took the doctor a moment to register the information.

"They are getting her set up in the NICU, then we'll have to schedule her surgery to be done right away. You should be able to see her very soon. I will send a nurse to get you once everything is ready. Do you have any other questions for me?" We were spent, and didn't have anything left to ask at that time. "It shouldn't be too long before you can see her. Hang in there. I know it's a lot to take in." With that, Dr. Pembroke turned away and started towards the door. "By the way, Blythe is a beautiful name. I'll be sure to have the nurses add it to her charts."

We spent the next thirty minutes just holding each other and trying to stay positive. Every time one of us would bring up something negative, the other one would attempt to shift gears. Then the nurse came in to bring us to the NICU. This was it; we would finally get to see Blythe. The nurse informed us that we would not be able to hold her, as she was attached to several machines, and the tubes would make it impossible. We could touch her, but that was it.

***

The elevator ride seemed to take forever, but eventually we heard the distinct ding as we came to a stop. The nurse escorted us to the left, and I could feel my heart start to race. I was both excited to see my new baby girl, and fearful of what might lie before me. My worries were eased the moment the nurse brought us to her bassinet. I looked at her sweet face, with those big brown eyes and cute button nose. She was perfect, and yet, she wasn't.

Emilie rolled her wheelchair up to see Blythe, and gently touched her belly. It was at that moment that she allowed herself to release her pain. The tears flowed freely, and her body shook and shivered as all of her sadness, frustration, and anger at the situation escaped her. She caressed her face, her head swollen with fluid that would lead to so many problems in the future. She reached out for me, and held on tightly with one hand, while the other carefully explored our daughter's tiny frame. It was then that we heard her cry for the first time. The sound was so amazingly beautiful; it changed our tears from ones of sadness, to those of incredible joy. We wanted nothing more than to hold her, but we knew that was not possible. We were left to simply admire her, telling her how much we loved her and how happy we were that she was finally there.

We had what seemed like only mere moments with her before we were told it was time for her to head back to surgery. Each of us took a turn leaning down and gently kissing her before they wheeled her bassinet away. The nurse escorted us back to our room, and told us they would let us know once she was all done and back in the NICU. While we continued to experience the stress of what could only be described as a certain type of loss, we pushed those feelings aside to focus on what we had actually gained. Our angelic little girl, Blythe Stevenson, was alive. No matter what might be physically wrong with her, she was still our daughter, and she would be loved.

***

The light was shining bright through the window in the nursery, falling softly on Blythe's face as she slept in her crib. I could hear her stirring, so I glanced at the screen to make sure she was okay. She was twitching a bit, but seemed to be fine. I rolled over to say good morning to Emilie, but was instead greeted by an empty space in our bed. I threw on my robe, put the small monitor in my pocket, and walked out to the living room. There she was, sipping on her tea, reading the latest book by her favorite author. The last few months had been so hard, learning to adjust to all that had to be done to take care of Blythe, but she was a master at it.

"Morning, sweetie", I said to the lovely image before me. "You're up early. Did you sleep okay?"

"Yeah, I just couldn't stay in bed anymore. Plus, I'm so close to being done with this book, I wanted to try and finish it before the busyness of the day started."

I could see she only had a few pages left in her book, but I had a feeling that was not the only reason she was up early. This day wasn't marked on the calendar, but it was marked in our minds. Three months had passed since our bundle of joy arrived. That time span was the average length of time that children with hydranencephaly survived. Blythe seemed to be doing just fine. In fact, the doctors would even say that she was thriving. She did have her issues; she was legally blind, couldn't hold her head up, and she had to be fed through a feeding tube. However, she was a happy baby, one who loved to be held and sang to. She loved to giggle, and she had a glowing smile.

I could feel the vibrations in my pocket just as I heard her crying. Emilie rose from her chair, placing a bookmark between the pages she was reading. "I've got her. Sit, relax. Finish your book." I turned towards the hall and walked down to the nursery. Realizing I must have forgotten to close her blackout curtains last night, I figured that the sunlight must have woken Blythe up. I reached into her crib, careful not to become tangled in her feeding tube, and raised her to my chest. I rested her head against my shoulder, taking care to support her neck with the extra weight it had to bear. I felt the silky strands of hair against my hand, and nuzzled my face to hers. Her crying settled down quickly. Blythe loved to be held. She craved touch from others. As I adjusted my hand on her neck, the scars that lingered there caught my attention. Two raised lines, almost perfectly symmetrical, side-by-side at the base of her head. One was there to save her life, the other, to decide when she was going to die.

Blythe received her microchip while in the hospital, just like every other newborn. Unlike most parents, we didn't take the time to worry about when our child's chip might be activated and she would die. We were fighting for each day already, hoping to make it to one week, then one month, then the dreaded three-month mark. Every day that she opened her eyes was a gift to us. Now we had reached a major milestone, and as I felt the scar from her chipping, a sense of dread came over me. Would our child have struggled and fought so hard to live, only to have her life cut even shorter through activation?

When Blythe was born, we were told that most babies born with hydranencephaly didn't make it out of the hospital. If they did, the parents should be prepared for them to die within the next few weeks. Making it to three months was such a major accomplishment, that the research articles all considered that the longest life span. Of course, there were cases of children who lived much longer, but the struggles that they went through were intense. Those cases were the outliers, not the norm. So there we were, at the three-month mark with our daughter, and we didn't know what might happen next. Emilie and I had counted each day as it passed, ticking it off like a check mark on an invisible calendar. We didn't want to talk about the passage of time, afraid that if we did, then our little dream world might come crashing down around us. It was obvious that we were both very aware as each day ended and a new one began. We had our own little celebratory smiles that we gave each other when we saw Blythe each morning. It wasn't a secret, yet neither of us ever spoke of it. That was not to say that we didn't honor the accumulation of days. We did acknowledge each week the first month, then the end of the second month, and of course, the third one as it arrived. The hourglass seemed to be sending grains of sand down just a little bit more slowly lately, but we didn't want to get our hopes up. We knew we had to make every moment count, simply because we didn't know when it would be our last one with her.

***

Emilie was gliding around the kitchen, softly singing as she gathered the ingredients to make Blythe's birthday cake. How was it possible that an entire year had passed already since she entered our lives? The fears that we had those first few months had all subsided, and we had just been enjoying the days as they came. We knew that Blythe's time with us was precious, and we knew it could end at any time. So on that day we would celebrate her, surrounded by friends and family who loved her. Emilie had started pouring ingredients into the mixing bowl, and as she danced back and forth between the counter and the refrigerator, I quickly stepped over to her and gathered her in my arms. With one of her hands in mine, and the other on her waist, we drifted across the tiles. She was smiling, laughing as I suddenly spun her around. She was not expecting it, and stumbled a bit, lightly crashing into the counter.

"Gerald, what are you doing? You know I am trying to get this cake made! We have so many people coming over, and I have so much to do. Can you please not make this any *harder* on me?"

Her smile quickly faded, and her surrounding glow disappeared. I knew she wasn't really mad at me, but that day was a hard one. As excited as we both were for that time, there was a dark cloud that hung over it. Just a few days earlier, a news story broke everywhere. Apparently, there was someone known simply as the Hacker who broke into Apeiron's computer systems. They were able to get access to the list of death dates that were in there, and they downloaded a copy of them. Now they were selling them for $50,000 each. We had been so thankful for every day we had with Blythe. When we were first told of her diagnosis, we thought we would lose her very quickly. As time went on, we just let the days pass, trying very hard not to focus on the passage of time, but still appreciating each moment. We knew that Blythe's life would be cut short from the hydranencephaly, but there was always the possibility that her death date would come earlier if her chip was set off. It wasn't a big focus for us previously, because we had no way of knowing when it would be. Now we had an opportunity to find out if she was programmed to die young, conceivably before the disease would take her.

I watched as Emilie continued to work on the cake. She never liked me being in the kitchen when she was baking, so I decided to head to my office and look over the cases I was working on now. One person was suing the other who hit their car at an intersection, another was going after their doctor for malpractice when they received a misdiagnosis, and a third was trying to get their company to pay for a work related injury. Being a lawyer definitely kept me busy, but I tried to make sure I made time for my family. There were many days when I didn't leave the office until seven or eight at night, only to come home and head straight into my office there to keep working. I made sure I ended up in bed next to Emilie each night, even if it was only for a few hours. My job took its toll on our family, but it paid the bills. With Blythe's diagnosis, our medical bills were quite large, even with the best insurance we could find.

Emilie never mentioned it, but I think she might have felt a bit of resentment towards me. After Blythe was born, I continued to work, but she had to leave her job as a teacher so she could stay home with our daughter. It was something she enjoyed doing, but she also loved being in the classroom. She was never given a choice in the matter. The variation between our salaries clearly indicated that I would return to work, and she would not. We had planned to put our daughter into daycare after Emilie's maternity leave time ended. We had gotten into the best one, applying the moment we found out she was pregnant. Those plans changed rather quickly. Now her days revolved around caring for Blythe and her many needs. Feeding her and flushing out her tube, making sure she doesn't lay for too long on one side so she does not get bedsores, and all of the other things that a mother does for her child. Even from my office, I could hear her moving around, making sure everything was perfect for this special day. Emilie did it all, and there were not enough words for me to express how thankful I was for her. My thoughts were interrupted as I heard her voice echoing through the intercom in my office.

"Hey, I need you to run out and get me more milk. I cannot believe we only had half of a container left! Please be quick about it, as I need to get this cake completely finished in the next hour."

"Sure, hun, I'll just grab my shoes and head out right now."

I turned off the light and gave Emilie a kiss goodbye as I headed to the hall tree to grab my shoes. Thankfully, the grocery store was only a few minutes away. I grabbed some milk, and picked up a bunch of flowers while I was there. Just a little something to show Emilie how much I appreciated her. When I walked back into the house, Emilie was sitting in a kitchen chair, a mess of ingredients on her shirt, a look of sheer exhaustion on her face. I put the milk in the fridge, handed her the flowers, and went to get a vase to put them in.

"Everything okay? You look absolutely whipped." I grabbed the blue and purple vase from the dining room hutch, and added some water to it.

"This should be the happiest day of the year, but I feel so weighed down. I am so…relieved, I guess, that we have gotten to this day with Blythe. I never could have imagined it a year ago. Yet I cannot help feeling as if we are about to head down the other side of a rollercoaster. None of these days are promised to us, and it seems like we have just been so lucky. I'm waiting for our luck to run out."

I sat down next to her, placed the vase on the table, and unwrapped the flowers so I could put them in the water.

"You're right, Emilie, we have been very lucky. But it doesn't mean our luck is going to run out." I was looking at her face to face now, and I could see the pain in her eyes. The last time I saw her looking this way was when we received the news of Blythe's diagnosis. I wasn't sure how to bring it up, so I just went ahead and blurted it out. "You know, if you're really that worried about it, we can always get in contact with the Hacker." Her eyes started to get much bigger, and she raised her hand to cover her mouth.

"Are you serious?!? What if we find out that she is supposed to live 30, 40, or 50 years, but then she dies in 6 months? How would you feel if we knew she had a chance to live longer, but this stupid disease kills her faster than that? Alternatively, on the other side, what if she continues to thrive, but we find out that her chip will be activated in the next year? What good would knowing that information do you?"

She was yelling at me by that point, clearly upset over what I had suggested. Her points were valid, but I didn't think that what I offered was that bad of an idea. If we found out that her death date was not until decades from now, it might give us some hope that she could live as long as this disease would allow her to. Instead of looking at it in a negative way, in a way that we would regret knowing, I was looking at it in a positive light. Knowing that the overseers wouldn't have a chance to take our daughter away from us before her life was simply destined to end was a relief.

Of course, there was the other side of knowing. If we found out that her chip would go off very soon, and she still had a chance at living, how would that change the way we were currently living? Would we try to get more out of each day? I thought that we already did that, since we knew her time was limited no matter what. I was having a hard time seeing a legitimate reason why we shouldn't reach out to the Hacker and find out. Then again, seeing how Emilie responded when I brought it up might be reason enough not to contact them. I certainly wouldn't want to upset her any more than I already had. Considering her feelings is something I always tried to do, but I couldn't just ignore my own feelings. This was definitely something that I would have to bring up again at a later date, and in a much more sensitive way. We didn't have a lot of time, so I had to start working on a plan right away. For that day at least, my focus would remain on my family, and the celebration for Blythe.

Emilie got back up to finish the cake. She was beginning to make the frosting while the cake baked in the oven. She had a natural talent when it came to baking. With so many people coming for the party, she was creating this amazing three-tier cake. The frosting would be purple, with butterflies created out of fondant resting on the individual layers. Of course, Blythe would not be able to see this wonderful creation, and she wouldn't be able to taste the deep, rich chocolate flavor that it contained. The party was more for us than it was for her, when it came down to it. I guess that's true for most one-year-old birthday parties, though.

***

As the last guests walked out the door, I turned to my amazing wife to congratulate her on a job well done. She seemed happy, but I could sense something else behind her smile. Something was stopping her from fully enjoying this day, poking at her brain and her heart.

"Emilie that was a fantastic party. From the decorations, to that gorgeous cake you made, you really pulled it off. Blythe was laughing a lot, so you know she enjoyed it, too. All of our guests seemed to have a great time. I'm super proud of you, and really appreciate all that you've done to make this a special day for Blythe."

I reached my arms around her waist and pulled her body into mine. Her muscles relaxed as she let herself settle onto my frame. Slightly turning my head, I inhaled the scent of her coconut shampoo, and then lightly placed my lips against her forehead. She slowly raised her head up, letting her mouth touch mine. I drew her in closer, using my tongue to part her lips so I could taste hers. I missed this so much. With the stress of this date approaching, I noticed that she pulled away more and more from me. I craved her touch. I needed it. I playfully lifted her off the ground and placed her back down. Without saying a word, I took her hand and led her to our bedroom. The room that once was filled with passionate moments between two young lovers, but had since become a cold place to simply lay our tired bodies down at the end of the day. I wanted that passion back, to feel the woman that I fell in love with 10 years ago.

Emilie didn't hesitate this time, quietly following my lead as we walked to the bedroom. She laid down next to me and ran her fingers through my hair. I peered at her longingly, but I didn't want to rush things. It seemed like forever since we had allowed intimacy to be a part of our lives, and things needed to move at whatever pace she was comfortable with. The lead was hers to take, as I ran my fingers along the curves of her side. She leaned in and kissed me, with a desire coming through so strong, I felt sparks tingling in my cheeks. Her hands were on my face, then my back, then the edge of my shirt as she pulled it over my head and tossed it on the floor.

The next hour was a blur of sights and sounds as we both gave in to our primal desires. I didn't realize how far apart we really were, until we finally came together. There were so many things I wanted to say to her, but I was so scared that I would ruin the moment.

"Blythe should be getting up from her nap soon. I'd better shower and figure out what dinner plans to work on." With that, Emilie got out of bed and proceeded to continue with the day.

"Um, okay. Why don't we go out for dinner? You've worked so hard today, let's just enjoy a night out."

"I don't know if the nurse will be able to come and stay with her on such short notice. It's just easier for me to throw something together."

"I understand. Do you want me to order something in? You deserve just to take it easy for the rest of the day. I was thinking maybe we could spend some time watching a movie together tonight on the couch once Blythe went to bed. You know, pop some popcorn and snuggle?" I was hoping that what we had just shared would be a turning point.

"Yeah, sure, let's get some Chinese food. I'll have the usual."

I wasn't getting the feeling that Emilie was excited about spending more time together tonight. It left me feeling confused, and to be honest, a bit lonely. In my mind, we had just broken through a barrier that had been slowly building for quite some time. I thought the closeness that we just shared was the turning point, and that perhaps we would start to return to a sense of normalcy between each other. At least some semblance of the shadows of the people that we used to be. I laid my head against the pillow and closed my eyes. What would it take to bring us back to where we used to be?

***

After Emilie and I took turns singing her favorite song to her several times over, Blythe was finally sleeping peacefully in her room. After a quick trip to the bathroom, I entered the living room to see Emilie sitting on the couch. I sat down next to her, and grabbed the blanket hanging over the back.

"Would you like to share?" I asked, offering an end of the blanket to her.

"Sure. I'll take some of that popcorn, too, if the offer still stands." She winked at me, and that charming smile was once again present on her face.

I handed her the blanket and went to throw a bag of popcorn in the microwave. I suddenly realized that I was humming away and appeared lighter on my feet. It appeared that Emilie was trying to round that corner, too, and maybe I just hadn't realized it. What seemed like mixed signals could simply be her trying while dealing with the stress of all that she has been going through lately. I was excited, but I knew that this was still on her timeline. I had to work hard to not let my enthusiasm take over and push her faster than she wanted to go.

I split the bag into two bowls and carried them to the coffee table, placing them down in front of her. Sitting back down onto the couch, she laid half of the blanket onto my lap, grabbed her bowl of popcorn, and handed me mine. Just as I grabbed the remote, she put her hand on mine.

"Before we start watching something, I wanted to talk."

I was not expecting this glitch.

"Okay, I'm all ears."

"I'm not sure where to start, so bear with me." She took a deep breath, and I could see her shoulders start to tense up. "When you brought up the idea of contacting the Hacker earlier, I know I was quick to respond in a negative way. I was so focused on making today special for Blythe, and I really felt like you were throwing this question at me from left field. I wasn't ready to talk about it, and I'm not really sure that I'm ready now, but I feel like it needs to be done." She turned more towards me, tucking one leg underneath the other one. Placing her bowl back on the table, she took my hand between both of hers. "I understand why you feel the need to find out Blythe's...activation date. I just don't know how it would make me feel. I struggle so much already, knowing that every moment I spend with her might be the last bit of time I get to share with her. Each smile, each giggle, each time she leans towards my hand when I go to pick her up, it could be the last experience we have. If we find out her date, how would that effect our day-to-day lives? Would we be happy to know that the plan might be for her to live a long life, and hope that she beats the odds and makes it to that point? Then how would we feel if she didn't beat the odds, and we knew that if she didn't have this disease, that she could have lived a longer life? Or the other side of the coin, if her date is set in the near future, and we see that she was doing okay on her own, only to have her life cut short? We work so hard to keep her as healthy as possible, and if the overseers took that away from us, how would you feel?"

Her voice was increasing at a rapid pace, and I could see that she was more upset than angry. By that point, her hands were no longer holding mine, but were instead flailing around as she tried to get her point across. I had been sitting there quietly, letting her say her piece without interruption. As she sat there, chest rising and falling quickly with each quick breath, I decided to interject, attempting to calmly respond to all that she had said.

"First off, thank you for discussing this with me. I apologize for coming at you earlier with this, not thinking about everything else you had going on at the time. I understand how confusing this all must be, and the decision is definitely not one to be taken lightly. I don't have the answers. If anything, I probably have more questions than anything else. My motivation in bringing it up today was simply the matter of time, or lack thereof. We only have one more week to submit our request to the Hacker if we want the information. After that, our decision is made for us. This is something that we have to choose together, and we have to agree upon. You've already stated the pros and cons for each side, so it really just comes down to us making the commitment either way."

Emilie seemed to have cooled back down, and she appeared to be intently listening to what I had to say. I wasn't sure there was anything else that I needed to say, though. I tried looking at her to see if I could read a response, but she was just looking at me in the same way. She suddenly got up and walked out of the room. I saw her turn down the hall, but I wasn't sure what she was going to do. She returned a minute later holding her laptop. She sat back down beside me on the couch, and started typing.

"I think we're ready to make a choice."

Part Three

Consequences

Chapter Twelve

<u>Eloise & Julian</u>

That last infusion was rough, even though physically nothing had changed. I had made up my mind, and was ready to live out my final days as they were meant to be. I was a little scared about how my body might feel during the time I had left, but my excitement for what the future could hold for Julian outweighed any of my fears. The universe smiled on me when not one, but two people who were previously interested in commissioning pieces from me replied that they still wanted them. With goals in mind, my attitude stayed positive, even when I didn't feel the greatest.

I knew that I couldn't change everything without Julian noticing, so I told him that I wanted to take a trip for our anniversary, and was planning a surprise for him. I explained that it was not a cheap vacation, so I was taking on the work to pay for it. He was not thrilled with the idea of me straining myself, but he understood that this was important to me, so he didn't try to fight me on it. Instead, he supported me by doing even more around the house, and making sure that I was able to rest when I wanted to.

When I spoke with my oncologist, I told them that I wanted to stop my treatments because I was done fighting. I was not about to mention the money being saved to find out Julian's death date. I couldn't imagine that any doctor would be okay with that being the justification for allowing yourself to die. They told me what would happen to my body, how it would slowly shut down as the cancer took over. They warned me that it was not the best option, but ultimately the choice was mine. We discussed medications that I could take to help with pain so that I would be as comfortable as possible. It would be difficult, but not impossible. That was all I needed to hear.

***

As the next week rolled around, Julian planned to accompany me to my appointment, not realizing that I was not going to truly be there. I had spent the week before dropping hints that I wouldn't mind the quiet time to myself, so when I asked him if he wouldn't mind staying home, it didn't take too long to convince him to remain there. He insisted on giving me rides there and back, though. After he dropped me off, I went inside the building and waited for him to leave. There was a little sitting area that I had seen many times before, so I strolled over there and sat down to read my book. Before I knew it, the four hours were over and I was walking outside to meet Julian back at the car. Week one down, three weeks to go.

The next two weeks were harder to convince him not to go with me. I came up with a few projects around the house for him to work on, and those kept him busy. Guilt took on a starring role in my performance, as Julian wanted to do anything that would make me happy. I had friends pick me up, giving them the excuse that I was working on a surprise for him and had rescheduled my time secretly to justify them not telling Julian I wasn't going to my appointments. It was a dangerous game that I was playing, but I was determined to win.

Before the final week arrived, I had reached out to the Hacker. I had managed to put away enough money to pay the fee without Julian realizing it. Since the infusion bills were set to auto draft from our account, he didn't realize that I had cancelled them and was taking the money out myself to put in my personal account. He still thought that I was planning a special trip, so when I put the money from my sculpture sales into my account instead of the joint one, he didn't bat an eyelash.

***

Between the stopping of the infusions, the extra strain on my body from making the sculptures, and the stress of keeping all of this to myself, I had become very weak. When the time came for my next infusion, Julian absolutely insisted that he go with me, and wanted to speak with the doctor about why I was getting worse. I couldn't come up with a reason in time to change his mind, so we left together. The entire ride there, I kept trying to come up with an excuse to have him leave. He was so focused on getting me better; all he did was talk about finding new ways to treat me. He was questioning why the medicines weren't working, and was adamant that we try new avenues.

"Julian, I need to tell you something", I said as we pulled into the parking lot.

"What's up? Is something wrong?" The way he was looking at me, I felt like he could see right through me and all of the lies I had been telling him.

"We can't go inside."

"Um, okay....and why not?"

"I'm not supposed to be here."

"What do you mean? Of course you are. You have the same appointment day and time every week." He was definitely getting confused now.

"I know, I just mean..." I really wasn't sure where to go with the conversation, so I stopped thinking and just let the words flow out like a river whose dam had just exploded. When I was done, he just sat there, chin pointed towards the floor, eyes closed. "Julian?" I don't know what I expected him to say, but I needed him to say *something*.

Instead, he simply started the car up, backed out of the space, and headed home.

We fought a lot over the next few hours, until my body just could not handle any more and I had to take a nap. I had already reached out to the Hacker, and the money was gone, so there was no point in really discussing it any further. Julian wanted me to go back on the infusions, but the doctor agreed with me that it wouldn't matter now, my days were numbered.

It was right around lunchtime when I woke up, so I walked to the kitchen to get some food once I wiped the sleep from my eyes. Julian was sitting at the table, already eating a sandwich. While not a big deal, this was unusual for him. We usually ate together, engaging in some sort of debate while enjoying our meal. It bothered me for half a second, but then I let it go, figuring he was just hungry and couldn't wait until I got up to eat.

"Hey, babe, I said to him as I crossed over to the cabinet to get a plate. He looked up at me, shook his head, and then went back to eating. "Are you seriously not talking to me now? Is this how today is going to go?" I thought I could put our earlier arguments behind us and move on. Choices had been made, and I saw no reason to linger on them any longer.

"What do you expect me to say to you? You have basically decided to kill yourself, and you didn't even speak with me about it! You are so fucking selfish!" Droplets of spit flew from his mouth as he screamed at me, something he never did before. I don't think I had ever seen him this angry before.

"I wouldn't have much longer to live whether I continued with the infusions for not. Instead of delaying the inevitable, I'm just letting it happen while giving you an opportunity at the same time. If anyone is being selfish, it's YOU!" So much for not fighting anymore today. Why couldn't he see that I was trying to help *him* for a change?

"Oh, so I'm selfish because I want to spend as many days as I can with the woman that I love? The one that means the world to me and I would do anything for? You know what then? Fine, consider me selfish!"

He slid his chair back so hard and fast it practically slammed into the rear wall as he stood up. With heavy steps, he walked to the front hall and grabbed his keys. Without another word, he opened the door and left. I didn't know where he was going, and that really worried me. We had never had a fight this bad before. I tried calling him right away, but he put it straight through to voicemail. This was awful.

About fifteen minutes later, I got a message from him stating that he was at the local coffee shop, and he'd be home in a while. He said he needed to calm down, and he would return once he was ready. While not thrilled with the situation, I was at least happy he was safe and sound. I responded that I understood and that I loved him. I finished my lunch and cleaned up. Not really having the strength to do anything else, I decided to make myself comfortable on the couch. I wasn't sure how long Julian would be, so I made the most of my time alone and picked up my book.

It was about an hour later when he returned, and he seemed to be in a better state of mind. He sat down on the sofa with me, but still didn't say anything. I leaned my body against his, hoping he would understand that this was my silent way of apologizing. I wasn't sorry for what I had done, but I did feel badly about how it made him feel. He tilted his head down so it rested on mine, and I knew that everything would be okay.

With him back, I decided to put my book away for a bit, so we could watch some television together. It was not long after that I felt myself drifting off to sleep. I vaguely remember Julian saying he was getting up to work on a painting as I felt his body raise up off the cushions. I felt his lips against mine as he moved towards his easel. I drifted off to a beautiful sleep, one that would last forever.

*The email from the Hacker arrived later that day, and Julian did open it, although there was a long pause before he did. He discovered that his death date wasn't for a very long time. Julian grieved for many days, not just for the loss of his wife, but also for the future he wasn't going to get to have with her. He was angry that she wouldn't get to experience the same things as him.

Using his emotions as a tool, he painted many projects over the next year. They were absolute masterpieces, and sold for a lot of money. He used those funds to pay for his trips to all of the places that he and Eloise had talked about going. While she wasn't there to hold his hand, he thought about her constantly, and never felt alone.

Chapter Thirteen

Asher & Silas

It had been several weeks since Silas and I shared our feelings for each other to the world through our social media accounts, and things were going great. After the initial excitement of the news wore down for everyone, we were left to just live our lives. A much more popular story had taken over now. The news was constantly filled with narratives about the Hacker, and the people who had changed their lives after finding out their death dates. As far as everyone knew, the overseers weren't any closer to finding out who the Hacker was, but more and more people were making wild guesses. You would be surprised how many people randomly concluded it was one of their friends or family members. Was it just suspicion, or money driven? While there wasn't anyone who didn't know about what the Hacker had done, no one seemed to want to take credit for it.

There was no way to avoid the constant barrage of news stories, articles, and social media postings about it. However, many people did their best to just ignore their new option and move on with their lives. Everyone talked about it, but I didn't know many people personally who had even thought about actually paying for it, let alone anyone who did find out their dates. It was a touchy subject, and you had to be careful whom you spoke freely to, never knowing how they felt or might judge you for your own opinions.

Personally, my life was going great. Since I won my award, I had started getting more offers for future projects. There were some absolutely terrible ones that I could not even get through reading, a few good ones I actually finished, and one or two that stood out as possibilities. Life seemed to be on the upswing for me, both in my career, and in my relationship. Silas was a loving, supportive partner who didn't mind that I had to spend hours reading through scripts. He loved taking on characters and performing cold readings with me. Most of the times he was just goofy, but sometimes the scenes we read were kind of hot.

***

It was how perfect my life seemed to have become that was the reason behind my reaching out to the Hacker. I was so scared that something would happen to me, that my death date would come early and ruin this perfect little world I had going on, that I had to find out. I already had a foot in death's doorway by being so much older than Silas, and I wanted to make sure that I would get to enjoy all of our time together. I wasn't worried as to what Sila's might be, as I had a feeling he was going to be around for a long time. However, it was important to me to find out his date as a sort of safety precaution. I knew I would have to accept whatever information I was given to me, so I didn't bother with hesitating. Once I had made the decision to contact the Hacker, I just had to sit back and wait.

The latency between the time I sent in my request and the when the answer arrived seemed like forever. In reality, it only took about twenty-four hours for the notification to arrive. Suddenly, first thing in the morning, it was there, the message that held the information detailing how long we had left to live. I wanted to open it immediately, but something held me back. I knew that I wanted the details; I didn't regret asking for them (or paying the hefty price tag to get them). I just was not sure what I was going to do once I found out. If I didn't have long, would I even bother to take on a new movie to direct? Would I rush things with Silas, trying to capture it all in a short period of time? Then I wondered if I would even bother telling anyone, especially Silas, what my death date was. Would I want them to know how much time they had left with me? Would it seem suspicious if I didn't tell them, but started changing the way I lived my remaining days? So many questions ran through my head.

I took a deep breath, and clicked on the link. A bunch of numbers and letters started scrolling down my screen very rapidly. I was informed that this would happen, so I wasn't too worried about it. Then everything went blank for a moment, and big red numbers popped up that took over the entire space. They flashed three times, and then froze there. After ten seconds, they were gone, and the screen returned to black. That was it. Those numbers were my future, and there was nothing I could do to avoid them. My destiny had stared at me, blinked its eyes, and then disappeared.

It took me a minute or two to fully process what I had just seen. I had my death date, but understanding how far away it was required a moment of processing. Once it hit me, I exhaled loudly and watched as black spots flashed throughout my field of vision. Apparently, I had been holding my breath while waiting and my head had gotten a bit dizzy. I was so relieved.

I. Had. Time.

There were forty-two years left in my life! I had enough time to get married and have kids! Enough time to direct more award winning films! Enough time to grow old with Silas! Now that I had seen my death date, I felt like the world was mine to conquer. I started to think about traveling, exploring the other quadrants and seeing what they had to offer. My mind raced with images and ideas of all of the wonderful things that I could still accomplish. Nothing felt out of my reach now. I was so elated that I had decided to find out, and I still had no regrets. With so much time, I didn't feel the need to tell anyone that I had been in touch with the Hacker. I didn't feel like there would be any glaring changes in my daily existence, nothing that would stand out from the ordinary life I have always lived. I kept the news to myself, just basking in the warmth that it had delivered to my heart and soul.

I was so lost in my head over finding out my own death date; I almost forgot to click on the link for Silas. My entire existence was in such a happy place, I didn't dare think that his news might not be so positive. Not wanting to jinx anything, I pushed all negative thought possibilities to the back of my mind, and clicked away without pause. Again, I watched as the numbers and letters scrolled quickly down my screen. I sat there impatiently for the second that all was blank. I felt the urge to look away as I saw red flash once more, but knew that I couldn't. If I didn't look, then I might not find out. After ten seconds, all would be lost and I would never have the chance to find out again.

Forcing my eyes to peer at what was in front of me, I had no way to avoid it.

One. More. Day.

My eyelids fluttered as I had a hard time believing what I was looking at. Silas' death date was *tomorrow*. How could that be? Was someone playing a trick on me? I tried clicking on the link again, but as was to be expected, it no longer worked. Maybe I had just read it wrong. My eyes were a bit watery, so maybe I had blurred the numbers when seeing them. It just was not possible that he had only one day left. I had *forty two freaking years* left! No, I simply wasn't going to believe it. I was positive that I had somehow gotten it wrong when reading the screen, but since I couldn't go back to view them again, I just had to trust my instincts. This simply was not right.

***

Whenever I was stressed over something, I would talk to Silas. I knew that I couldn't speak to him about this, as I did not intend to tell him what I saw. Not really believing it was true, there was no reason to stress him out about it. Why should I put the fear of dying tomorrow into him, when it was all just a mistake? I knew that he would be at the gym for the better part of the morning, so I waited a couple of hours before calling him.

"Hey, do you want to grab some lunch? I've been starving all morning. Stupid protein smoothies just aren't doing it for me anymore."

"Aw man, I would love to, but I have to work. I promised Felix I would cover his shift today. You know, us simple folk have to work in between the big jobs to pay the bills", he said jokingly.

"That sucks, but I understand. What time do you get off work?"

"Not until nine. I'll have to rush home and feed Lancelot, but I can come over and hang out afterwards if you'd like."

"That works. Just give me a shout when you're on your way."

"Okay. I've gotta run and get ready for work. I'll see you tonight."

"Have fun at work!" I hung up the phone, and immediately felt guilty for saying that. I knew that Silas hated his job. I had enough money to support the both of us, but he was a proud man, and he wouldn't even let me pay the bill two times in a row when we went out. I appreciated that about him, along with so many other things.

The day went on as usual, and I started to get more and more nervous as nine o'clock drew closer. I found myself conflicted between wanting to act as if I hadn't gotten a combination of both the most wonderful and terrible news this morning, and grabbing Silas the moment he walked in my door, never letting him go. I still had a hard time believing that the death date I saw for him was indeed real, but I was trying to come to terms with the possibility that it was. If my eyes had not been deceiving me, and I wasted our last moments together pretending that they had, then I would be racked with guilt forever.

When it came down to it, I gave Silas a big hug when he came inside, but then let him go so I could fix us both a drink. I listened as he talked about how shitty work had been, and how he was hoping I would start on a new movie soon so he could quit his job. The words coming out of his mouth were nothing more than mere movements of his lips, as I hard time focusing on what he was actually saying. All I could do was stare at him and smile, trying to take in everything as it was happening.

We sat there for a while, enjoying each other's company along with several drinks apiece. Before we knew it, the grandfather clock in the hall was chiming the start of a new day. The next day. Silas' *last* day.

"Wow, is it really midnight already? Where did the last few hours go? I feel like all I've done is sat here and complain." I didn't care if he was complaining, I was just happy that he was here.

"If they were in those bottles, then I would say the hours were in our bellies now." I laughed at my own stupid joke, trying to keep the mood lighthearted.

"At least I don't have to work tomorrow. I don't think I should be driving for a while, either. Mind if I crash here tonight?"

"Seriously? Of course, I don't mind. I'll do my best not to hog the blankets." This time Silas laughed with me. I loved his laugh, it was just a bit higher in pitch than his speaking voice, and it always made me laugh even more.

I gathered up our glasses and put them in the sink to be dealt with tomorrow. There would be time for that later on. The clock's toll had sounded like death itself reverberating through the room. I didn't want to go to sleep. Any minutes with my eyes closed would be considered wasted time. What if I fell asleep, and when I woke, Silas was already dead?

"Hey, by any chance do you have a toothbrush? My mouth is kind of dry and funky feeling, and while there are many things I may share with you, a toothbrush is not one of them."

I always kept some spare essentials in the house, so I offered Silas a toothbrush while giving him some privacy in the bathroom. After a few minutes, he came back out again. He had gotten comfortable while in there, and when he came out he had nothing on but a pair of boxer briefs. They hugged his body in all the right places, and I suddenly could not wait to get into bed.

"I'm going to wash up. Feel free to make yourself comfortable." I gestured towards the bed and headed into the bathroom to get myself cleaned up. As I looked back, I could see him rubbing his hands on the sheets. I used only the highest thread count, and I was glad someone else was going to enjoy them with me.

As I approached the bed, Silas patted the spot next to him, inviting me to snuggle up. I practically jumped in, sending the pillows bouncing up in the air.

"What's with the shirt? You hiding something?" Silas asked me as he grabbed a hold of my undershirt.

"Not everyone has a six pack underneath theirs. I'm not used to sharing my jelly belly with others." I tried to shake off the negative feelings that were coming on, but I had always been self-conscious about my body. I wasn't fat, but I certainly wasn't as toned up as he was.

"Jelly belly? Whatever. You are beautiful and sexy. If I didn't want to be with you, *all* of you, I would not be here. Now, let's get rid of that." He reached over and started pulling my shirt above my head. I relented, and attempted to smile as he revealed my glaring insecurities.

He gingerly kissed my neck, working his way down my chest, until his mouth rested on my stomach. My abs were starting to hurt as I did my best to suck in and appear flatter than I was. He laid his head down on my belly, encircling his fingers in the little hairs that led down my happy trail. The moment was near perfect, but I couldn't escape my own head. I could hear the ticking of the clock, and I felt like The Tell Tale Heart was beating in my brain. Every moment became a picture that I would try and mentally frame, just in case it was the last one.

The worst part was that I was experiencing all of this on my own. Without having told Silas about the information I possessed, I had to act as if everything was normal. I doubted my choice every second, but I could never fully justify sharing it with him. At this point, it was too late, and I had to suffer in silence. I would deal with this pain alone, the results of my choice to find out.

I gently pulled Silas up so that his eyes met mine. Running my fingers through his hair, I drew him closer to me and laid my lips upon his. There was a newfound passion between us, sparks lighting up the nerve paths that ran throughout my body. I couldn't get enough of him, trying to take in every sight, every sound and smell that emanated off his figure. Our own bodies, the yin and yang, fit together to form a perfect union.

As we laid in bed, sweat slowly dripped down every inch of me. My instincts told me to get up and take a shower, but I feared leaving him alone. I looked over and noticed that his eyes were closed, and he had fallen asleep. I lingered next to him, watching his chest rise and fall with each breath. There was a towel nearby, so I simply grabbed that and wiped myself down. Tossing it onto a nearby chair, I curled my body around Silas' and gave in to the exhaustion that was pulling at me. I couldn't stop the hands of time from slowly reaching out to take him away, but I wouldn't let them steal the moments I had left.

Chapter Fourteen

The Blank

I reached up on the tips of my toes and grabbed a ripe peach from the tree branch above me. I took a second to admire its beauty before biting down into it, letting the juices drip down my chin and onto the ground below. It was hard to believe that just three years ago that ground was so dry, I wasn't sure if I would be able to survive much longer with the way it was withering away. Then the soil became moist and fertile, providing me with everything I needed for my farm and myself. I grabbed another peach and pulled out my knife, ready to cut a slice out for Trevor. Then I remembered that he was no longer there, and my heart dropped. It had been a few months since he passed away, peacefully lying on the couch, his favorite place to be. His absence saddened me beyond compare, but I was thankful for the time we had together. That boy provided me with my sanity sometimes when I thought it was all but gone.

The sun was shining brightly in my eyes, interrupting my thoughts for the moment. I had to squint while gathering the day's bounty from my orchards, gently placing each piece of fruit into the handwoven basket I had made so many years before. That day was a leisurely day, and I enjoyed the warmth on my skin as I took my time striding through the groves. A few birds could be heard overhead, but other than that, it was generally quiet. The kind of peace that settles calmly into your soul.

That inner tranquility was suddenly jarred as I heard a whirring sound in the distance. I looked up and saw, to my horror, a helicopter quickly descending from the skies above. It was out of control, and I could tell that it was not about to stop before hitting the ground. There was a very loud explosion, and a big puff of smoke rose through the air as the failing piece of machinery crashed into the soft terra firma below. It was difficult to judge distance, but I took off towards the direction I thought it was, not sure what I was expecting to see or do once I got there.

***

Out of breath, I arrived at the scene about ten minutes later, and was immediately overcome with alarm and panic. The helicopter was mangled, smoke rising out of it so thick it was hard to see inside. The flames had already started to die down, but I could see that someone was still trapped inside. In a twist of luck, they had come down right near the lake, and I rushed over to gather water. I didn't have anything on me to collect it with, but I found a piece of metal from the crash that was cooled down enough for me to pick it up. The way it had bent, I was able to use it in a manner similar to a small bowl. I rushed back and forth from the lake, attempting to put out the remaining flames. The man inside was injured beyond repair, and I knew his chance at life had been extinguished long before the flames were.

As I sat there trying to take in what had happened, allowing myself a moment to breathe, I thought I heard something off to my left. I quickly scrambled towards where the sound was coming from, and was shocked to discover a woman lying in the grass, mostly obscured by a large rock, several hundred feet away. She was badly injured, but she was alive. She appeared to be drifting in and out of consciousness, and the few words she was able to say didn't make much sense. I told her to lie still, and that I would be getting help.

Already worn out from all of that running, never mind the sheer exhaustion of the situation at hand, I gathered what little energy I had left and headed back to the house. I grabbed a few light blankets (one was Trevor's, his energy was needed now), some homemade bandages, snacks, and a couple of jars of water, and sprinted towards the boat. Tossing everything inside, I started fiercely paddling in the direction of where the crash site was. When I got there, I was happy to see that the woman was still alive.

I did a quick scan of her body to try to determine the extent of her injuries, at least on the outside. She didn't have many burns on her, thankfully. It appeared that she was thrown from the helicopter during the explosion. She had some nasty wounds, so I covered those the best that I could with the bandages I had brought. I tied off any areas where there was blood flowing, wrapped her up very gently in the blankets to provide warmth, and carried her to the boat. There was barely enough space for me to lay her down, leaving her feet pressed right up against the back edge. She still wasn't saying much, but I kept talking to her, reassuring her that we were going to get her help.

My body went into autopilot, a repetitive refrain of *forward-middle-back* as I pushed the waters behind me. My mind, on the other hand, was zipping from thought to thought like a cat pouncing on shadows as they danced among the sunbeams. What caused the helicopter to crash? Who were the people inside? What was it doing in that airspace? What am I going to do with the body of the deceased person? What am I going to do with the woman in my boat? What happens when I get to town?

All of these years living off the grid; my biggest worry was how to take care of myself and survive on my own. Now I was suddenly taking responsibility for a total stranger, and one whose life was hanging in the balance. What was I thinking?!? I knew that it would take me well over a day to get to civilization, even if I paddled non-stop. Holding this woman's life in my hands, I knew I had to come up with a plan on how to get her there safely. I kept going for as long as I could muster, keeping an eye on her and periodically checking to make sure she was doing okay. I kept cranking my hand lantern to try to give me light as the sun set and the stars came out. Eventually, my arms kept locking up with cramps, and I had to give in to my fatigue. I steered the boat towards the edge of a section of land, and tied it up to a nearby tree. I cradled the woman in my arms and carried her over to a spot with clear grounds and plenty of surrounding trees to provide a canopy. Still wrapped in the blankets, she was shivering a bit, leading me to believe that she might have been starting to go into shock. I helped her drink some water, pouring the liquid between her parched lips, attempting to keep dehydration off the list of problems. I laid down near her, close enough to keep her warm, but not enough to exacerbate any existing injuries. I closed my eyes, surrounded by the stars and fears of what tomorrow would bring.

***

The next morning, I awoke and immediately looked over at the stranger beside me. Thankfully, I could still see the blankets rise and fall over her chest. My biggest fear put to rest; I knew we had to start the second half of our journey right away. I carried her to the boat, untied it, and set us on our voyage. The waters remained calm, giving me a little bit of confidence that today might be favored. We traveled all day, continuing on through the night hours once again as we edged closer and closer to the people I had left behind so many years ago. I was overcome once again, all strength depleted from my body as the time dragged on. I knew we were close, so I pushed through, even if our pace suffered because of it.

Just when I thought I couldn't possibly go any further, I saw the lights of a town coming through the trees of a nearby piece of land. I steered the boat towards what I hoped was not a hallucination, and found a place to bring it ashore. Looking up a small incline of a hill, I could see a building that was lit up inside.

I didn't want to leave the woman in the boat alone, but it was only a short walk away, and I knew that this might be my only chance at finding her help. Not sure if she could even hear me at this point, I told her that I would was going away for just a minute to try to find someone who could provide her aid. I figured that since it was still pretty dark out, she was safe under the cover of night.

As I walked towards the building, I had a flashback to when my roommate, Antonio, first came back from getting his microchip. The way he was so insistent that the overseers were trying to kill us all, and how they would decide on when you would die. I remembered the details he gave me regarding the sensors, and how they would know if someone didn't have their chip. Suddenly I found myself stopped dead in my tracks, paralyzed by the fear of being found out. If I walked into that building, would I set off a sensor for not being chipped? Would some alarm start ringing loud enough for everyone to know, sending rule enforcers rushing to my side to bring me in? I had a choice to make, and it wasn't an easy one.

Would I risk giving up my own life in order to save someone else's?

There were so many scenarios spinning around my brain, and none of them had endings that I felt 100% comfortable with. I thought about all of the time and effort I put into saving this woman. I had physically bankrupt my body to get her to safety, and I didn't even know who she was, or if she would make it. I shook my head, hoping to get the thoughts to settle down inside and continued my steps toward the light. As I got closer, I could see that it was some kind of twenty-four hour convenience store. The likelihood that there were sensors in the doorway was very strong. This was my moment, press on, or turn back.

I will admit it, I got scared. I turned on my heels and went back to where I had left the woman. I couldn't risk being discovered, but I still had to get her taken care of. Ever so slowly and delicately, I unwrapped the blankets from around her body. I didn't need her to have anything on that could connect her to me. Hoisting her up for the last time, I could hear her moan softly as the pain must have coursed through her body. My steps were made to tread softly so as not to be located, getting nearer to the store with each one. Finally, I placed her within reach of the bottom stair, resting her head towards the light so she could be seen. I started towards the boat, using the darkness as my protector. After a few steps, I called out for help, hoping someone would hear me and come to her rescue. As I got further away, the sounds of distant footsteps running in that direction rang in my ear. I felt that she was safe, and now it was time for me to be as well.

***

It took me about three full days to get back home, as I wasn't in as much of a rush this time, and I will still working on replenishing my energy. Thankfully, there were some fruit and berry trees lining parts of the shoreline to help provide me with more nourishment along the way. Tired, but beyond thrilled to be done with that adventure, I tied up the boat and proceeded to walk towards the house. I still wasn't completely self-assured with my final decision, but what was done was done. It was time to move on, and I was ready to start by getting a good, long rest in.

As I got closer to the house, I immediately noticed the change in the landscape. There were several cars there, and a lot of people milling around. How could I forget? I still had a dead man not far from my property, and his chip must have been flagged for inactivity the last few days. I barely had time to take it all in before I heard someone yelling and saw them pointing in my direction. Two men jumped in a car and started driving towards me, while another man and a woman came at me on foot. I knew I wasn't going to be able to outrun them, so I just stood there and raised my hands to the skies. Within moments, the car stopped and all four people were soon by my side. They grabbed my wrists, pulled my arms behind my back, and led me away.

Everything that I had worked so hard for, all that I had become on my own would be no longer. The house would eventually be torn down, the crops burned, and the animals taken to the mainland farms. When I returned to the town, they immediately chipped me and sent me off to a work camp. I was given a sentence of 75 years, which meant I would never get out. The only hope I had left was that my death date would come soon. Now I lived to work, no longer working just to live. I was ready to be activated.

Chapter Fifteen

The Stevensons

Making the decision to message the Hacker came easier than I had expected once we had openly expressed our feelings with one another. Blythe was the most important thing in both of our lives, and we had dedicated our worlds to keeping hers going. We feared that we would get the worst news once we read the message, but neither of us was sure exactly what that was. An early date? A late date? We couldn't decide which one we had preferred to see.

We could have backed out of viewing it if we had wanted to. Just because the information would become readily available to us, it did not mean we had to actually click on the link and find it out. There were going to be consequences for our choice, and we thought we had considered them all before even sending the Hacker their payment. Still, no one ever knows exactly what will happen once they get life altering news.

Emilie and I held each other's hands as the numbers appeared before us. She let out a little squeak as she forcefully inhaled sharply. Our baby girl had just turned one year old, and now we knew how much longer she might have at a chance for living. The disease was still our main concern, not the activation of her chip. I breathed a sigh of relief, not realizing how strongly I had wanted this to be the outcome.

"How are you feeling?" I asked Emilie, not sure what her reaction signified.

"Honestly, I guess I'm happy. She may not live as long as we'd like her to, but we know that it won't be someone else's decision as to when her life does eventually end."

"I understand, and I feel the same way. We can't choose how long she gets to live, but it's nice to know that, even with the circumstances being such difficult ones, no one else will have chosen that for her, either."

I really had thought that I wasn't leaning towards either answer prior to seeing the details of her death date. Emilie and I had discussed (sometimes a little bit too noisily) all of the talking points. When all was said and done, we knew a true answer could never be found. Blythe wasn't just a bunch of questions and answers, she was our daughter. Now we knew that she would be with us as long as this disease will allow her to be.

We hadn't told anyone that we were going to ask the Hacker, so we didn't see the need to let anyone know about this newfound information. This news would just be something special between us, a sacred bond that would allow us to live our lives just a bit more easily. If someone were to question us in regards to whether or not we looked into it, we would lie and say there was no need since we knew we had limited time with Blythe already. On the outside, it looked as though we had it all together, even if the pieces were crumbling internally.

***

The day after we received the news, Emilie and I had been talking about some short-term plans we would like to do as a family. It seemed that by knowing she wasn't going to be activated any time soon, we suddenly felt like we had forever and a day to be with her. Her medical issues still gave us limitations, but we were going to continue to make the best of it, and work even harder to make things better.

It was during one of these conversations that I had a sudden realization. While we were no longer concerned about the overseers taking Blythe from us, we had failed to think about them taking *us* from *her*. What if one of our death dates was to happen while Blythe was still alive? Could just one of us handle raising her? If I were to die, Emilie would have the money from my death benefits, but that would run out quickly with Blythe's medical expenses. If Emilie were to die first, I'm not sure how I would be able to take care of Blythe while still working. We were so focused on our baby girl being there for us, we didn't take the time to stop and think about us being there for her.

"Emilie, we need to figure out what we want to do when it comes to our death dates. We've put all of our attention on keeping

Blythe safe, but what good is it if we're not here to enjoy this life with her?"

"Oh god, you're right! How did we not think about that? You need to reach back out to the Hacker and get our dates!" I could hear the fear rising in her voice as the color in her cheeks began to drain away.

"I'll go and do that right now, don't worry. I'm sure it will all be fine. We were so worried about Blythe's date, and it all worked out. Have confidence, and keep thinking positive thoughts."

I went to my office and sat down at my computer. My chair felt more stiff than usual, a general sense of discomfort taking over my body. Logging into my messaging account, I quickly composed a note to the Hacker. My fingers flew across the keyboard, trying to convey our desperation through a combination of letters strung together. It took me less than a minute from start to finish, sending the memo on its way.

We knew from our first experience that it can take up to twenty-four hours to get a response, but that didn't stop us from checking the inbox early. Emilie was reading Blythe a story when I went to look, just one hour later, to see if there was a reply. In my heart, I didn't expect it to be there, but I was getting antsy and had to at least look into it.

Imagine my surprise when I saw that we had received a return message already! I called Emilie through the intercom, and she walked in holding Blythe. Together, they sat down on the couch next to my desk. I could barely speak, so I turned my screen towards them and pointed, hoping she would understand. Her eyes lit up, and she told me to go ahead and open it.

As hysterical as we were when it was time to open up the email about Blythe, this was even more nerve wracking. My hand was shaking as I tapped the button and watched the screen change before me. The message opened, but there wasn't a link inside. In fact, there was only one word there for us to see.

EXPIRED

What? I was flabbergasted. Not knowing what it was that I was looking at, I closed the message and went back to my inbox to see if perhaps I had clicked on the wrong one. I tried it again.

EXPIRED

The word stared back at me with such intensity; I could feel my eyes burning. A wave of nausea swept through my body as I began to understand what was going on.

"Emilie, what day is it?"

"Um, it's Tuesday. Why?"

"No, the date. What is today's date?"

"The fifteenth. What's going on?" She was getting noticeably upset, and I wasn't sure how to break the news to her that had just clicked in my head. I slumped down in my chair, my chin resting on my chest. "Gerald, you're scaring me. What is it?"

"Yesterday was the expiration date for making requests to the Hacker." I hated hearing the words as they came out of my mouth almost as much as I did saying them. "We missed the cut off, and now we won't be able to find out what our death dates are."

253

I was devastated, and I could tell that Emilie was, too. We had put ourselves through such an emotional roller coaster recently, and now the attraction was shut down before we got our final joy ride in. I closed my computer, joined Emilie and Blythe on the couch, and just held them.

Chapter Sixteen

Adelaine Kingston

There were moments when time seemed to race by, and others when it trudged along like a snail climbing uphill. Amazingly, over the course of that month I had only received 11 requests from people wanting to buy their death dates. While that may not seem like a lot, it meant changing each one of those lives individually, along with how those changes affected the rest of the population. It also meant that I was financially stable for once in my life! I didn't want to run the risk of being suspicious with all of my newfound money, so I kept my purchases to a low amount. I bought myself some new clothes, ate out at nicer restaurants (and left bigger tips), and bought a few impulse items. I tried to spread out my expenses in different places so no one would see me spend too much at one time. I definitely lived it up, but within reason. I still had bills to pay, and I wanted to make sure that I was able to continue staying on top of them while enjoying some of the finer things that life had to offer. I had expected more people to respond, but I guess between the cost and the doubt that people continued to have, the amount who showed an interest was bound to be limited.

My job still took over most of my time, and it was interesting to go in each day and hear the chitter chatter from my coworkers as they discussed the latest breaking news on the Hacker. It was really hard in the beginning to not say anything, but I knew that if I dared give away even the slightest hints, I put myself at risk of being discovered. As the days and weeks wore on, I managed to take in what they were saying and let it fade away. My number one concern was always protecting myself, so everything I said or did revolved around that. At the end of the workday, about three weeks into my delivery of the death dates, one of my coworkers started up a conversation with me as we were shutting our computers down.

"Hey Del, you haven't said much when it comes to the Hacker. What are your thoughts? Do you believe they're really giving people their death dates?" It was hard to tell where Sebastian was coming from. I really tried not to engage in conversations with the others on my team, so I usually kept my part of the discussion to short answers.

"Who knows? I think that if someone was willing to pay that much money to find out, then you would hope that they were getting the real information sent to them." Okay, not too much detail, but hopefully that would satisfy his curiosity.

"Yeah, you would hope so. But what do *you* think? How honest do you think this Hacker person truly is? I mean, how did they even get access to the files to begin with? I'm sure the overseers have everything pretty tightly locked up, don't you?" Oh, Sebastian, if you only knew.

"I just write code for games, so I don't know much about security systems. When it comes to how honest they are, I have no clue. I try to see the good in everyone, so I'd like to believe that if they really do have the numbers, then they're trying to get them out there for a good reason." Okay, it was time to end this conversation. "It's been a long day, and my brain is fried. I'm going to head home, eat some dinner, and veg out for the night. Have a good one, Sebastian. I'll see you tomorrow." I grabbed my bag and headed towards the door.

"Oh, alright. Goodnight, Del. Drive safely. See you tomorrow!"

I waved goodbye to him, and walked out and down the hall to the front exit. Sebastian was a sweet guy, and he was easy on the eyes, too. I never noticed him showing an interest before, but lately it seemed as if he was almost going out of his way to start a conversation with me. Maybe I was imagining it, letting paranoia get the better of me. Besides, even if he were interested in me, now would not be a good time to start anything with anyone. My focus was on me, and I could not share that with someone else without feeling as if I was putting myself at risk.

When I got home that night, my mind couldn't stop thinking about Sebastian. What if I wasn't just being paranoid? What if he really was trying to get information out of me? Was it possible that he suspected that I was the Hacker? I could tell that I was spiraling, so I decided to take Trixie for a long walk to try to clear my head. Everywhere I went; it seemed that people were whispering about me. Well, not me specifically, but the Hacker, who they didn't know just happened to be me. The more I listened to what was being said, the more I felt their eyes upon me. My heart began to race and I felt a panic attack coming on. I hurried home, tugging at Trixie's leash to get her to move faster.

Closing the door behind me and locking it, I sat down on the floor and tried to take in slow, deep breaths. Trixie kept trying to crawl into my lap, sensing that something was wrong. Her fur was tickling my nose, and it made me laugh, helping me to calm down. After a few minutes of snuggling my matted little hairball, my heart rate returned to normal and I could breathe properly again. That was just one of the many times that I was thankful to have Trixie in my life. She had saved me more times than I could count, and I didn't know what I would do without her.

It was getting late, so I called the food delivery service to pick up some dinner for me. By the time it arrived, I had already changed into some more comfortable clothes and was flipping through the television apps to see what would catch my eye for the night. My doorbell notification went off, so I went and got my order and sat down at the kitchen table to eat. As I unpacked the containers, I realized they forgot my French fries. Damn, what good is a burger without fries? Disappointed, but too hungry to deal with it, I just scarfed down what I had and cleaned up. With nothing appealing to me on the t.v., I started up a video game and played until I was ready to call it a night.

***

The next day at work, Sebastian tapped my shoulder as I was getting ready to head out for lunch. "Hey, where ya headed?"

"I'm just going to Stefano's to get a sub. Why, what's up?"

"Oh, nothing. I was just wondering if you wanted some company. I was gonna grab some lunch, too."

"Um, sure. Come on."

I figured it wouldn't be a big deal to have him join me, unless I made it a big deal.

Off we went, heading to get some lunch together. Nothing weird to see there, nothing at all.

We got our food and sat at a small table inside the restaurant. Our conversation flowed naturally, talking about the latest projects we were working on at Prothymos. There were a few quiet gaps here and there, but no long awkward silences. I enjoyed the time we spent together, but I wasn't unhappy to return to work and get back to doing my job. My mind was still focused on keeping my social circle small, protecting myself at all costs.

About an hour later, I got a text from Franklin asking if I wanted to go to the bar that night with him and Sebastian. Oh yeah, I had forgotten that the two of them were buddies outside of work. I politely declined, saying that I was starting to get a headache and was just going to take the night easy and rest up once I got home. The truth was that I was feeling just fine, but I was beginning to worry. Franklin introduced me to the Underground. Did he show it to Sebastian, too, or vice versa? Did Sebastian know that I knew about it? Was that why he was suddenly spending more time with me?

After work, I spent hours going through all of my files and accounts, double and triple checking things to make sure they were secure. What if I had slipped somehow and now there was someone out there who had figured out who I was? Could Franklin be suspecting that I was the Hacker since he knew that I was looking into the Underground? Did he bring up his suspicions to Sebastian, and now they were both questioning the possibility? All of these questions started swirling around my brain, and I truly began getting a headache. I took some meds and went straight to bed. Tomorrow would provide me with a clearer perspective.

***

The next couple of weeks came and went, and my fears of being found out grew even more intense. As the last death date was sent out, I shut down all of my accounts. I was sure to delete any and all traces of things I had used, but there was always a sense of doubt in the back of my mind. I had been hearing things that I wasn't sure were actually being said. I felt the stares of citizens as I walked the streets, their eyes conveying a knowing sense of something within me. I was always in a heightened state of panic, and I could not find a way to get it to come down. My fears were taking over, breaking me down inch by inch. I had to get away; I had to go where no one knew me.

I started by taking short trips to different parts of the Beta quadrant, since that was where I grew up, and the only areas I really knew how to get around. I packed a small bag and found a few places where I could take Trixie with me to stay. Getting out of my house was definitely beneficial. I traveled around and explored sights that I had heard of, but never been to. The air felt fresher as I focused more on investigating nature instead of trapping myself inside. Still, I couldn't shake the feeling that people knew my secret. There was no concrete evidence I could point to that verified it, but I continued to experience a sort of psychosis. If someone looked my way, I would swear that they were checking me out, planning on how they were going to turn me into the overseers. Every conversation I overheard seemed to make mention of the hack. My part was done, and now was the time I should be enjoying the fruits of my labor. Unfortunately, it was hard to fully appreciate the rewards when my anxiety was only increasing.

While I enjoyed my time away, it never seemed long enough. I always had to come back after a few days, not being able to miss too much work at one time. I would feel refreshed upon my return, but the feeling would not last. Within a day or two of being back, the perception of being trapped in my own mind would commence again. I realized that these mini vacations, although helpful during the time I was on them, were not the solution. I needed a bigger change.

The first step was deciding on where to go. Having never been outside of the Beta quadrant, I had to do some research to see what was even out there. Every quadrant had places within it that seemed like they would be enjoyable to venture to. When mapping out my travels, it became clear to me what would be the best way to get around everywhere with Trixie. I found someone local that was selling a travel trailer that my car could pull. It wasn't too big, which made it easy for me to drive with no prior experience. Having a little house on wheels meant I could pretty much go anywhere I wanted. There was plenty of room for Trixie, and based on her reaction to our mini trips, I knew she would be excited to take to the open road.

I came up with a basic outline of where we would go, but I didn't want to limit myself. If I was relishing my time in one location, I wanted to be able to stay there until I was ready to leave. To the same affect, if I was uncomfortable somewhere, the freedom to just get up and go was important to me. This was my chance to start fresh, giving myself a new beginning and leaving behind all that was weighing me down. I would no longer be the Hacker. I didn't even have to be Del anymore if I chose not to be!

I told my boss at Prothymos that I didn't want to quit, but that I needed some time to myself for a mental health break. Thankfully, they could see that I had been struggling, and they granted me a temporary leave. I terminated my contract for my home, having to pay a small fee for ending it early. I made sure that I did not provide anyone with more details than were necessary in regards to why or where I was going. The hardest part was leaving my family behind. My explanation to them was just that I wanted to explore the quadrants while I was still young enough to appreciate them. I told my mom that I had been saving up money when she asked how I could afford to do that. Both she and Davina wished me the best after I promised that I would check in with them periodically to let them know that I was safe.

Everything was in order and I was ready to go. I picked up a copy of the local paper to have some reading material along the way. There was a story in it about the death dates, but it was at least halfway through the issue. I was not front-page news anymore. It seemed that the world was ready to move on from what I had done, and so was I.

Epilogue

My name is Hugo, and I am one of the overseers. I am putting my own life at risk by putting this information out there, but I feel that it is necessary. Being one of the people who has to keep the secrets of the quadrants is very stressful. We are trained to monitor so many things, yet we can only talk about what we find with other overseers. None of the things that we find out can be mentioned to our family or friends. It really weighs you down. I have worked as an overseer for more than ten years, and the things that I have seen and heard during that time would shock you to your core. I managed to hold it all inside, every bit of it, until now. I always wondered if I had a breaking point, and when this last action was taken, I knew I had found it. The time has come to tell my story.

The microchipping system was created in order to control the population of the four quadrants. While there were many people who were against it (even amongst the overseers), it was decided that the use of that program was the best way to keep our resources in check.

Things had gotten distressing around the world, and there was a lot of research and discussion done to try to find ways to improve the current situation. The groups that argued against microchipping fought against the humanity of it, but they could not argue against its effectiveness. We might not have survived as a whole if we didn't implement it when we did.

　　We were all scared as we went to get the procedure done. We never knew when our loved ones would die beforehand, but suddenly it seemed like their lives (and our own) had an expiration date that didn't exist earlier. With everyone's information collected, maintaining the database became a constant job. We had an entire department dedicated to assigning the new dates to each life as it entered the world. Then there were the workers who focused on the updates as people passed away through unexpected circumstances. It took a lot of work, and it was all very time consuming.

　　Some of the top minds from each quadrant created our security system. They spent weeks designing the methods that would be used to protect the information. The overseers controlled all of the files, so the safeguarding of it was not taken lightly. We had people practice attempting to break in, guaranteeing (or so we thought), that it was foolproof. No one could have foreseen what would happen, or the consequences of the actions that would be taken.

I remember coming into work the day after the Hacker broke in. Everyone was running around, crazily trying to figure out exactly what had happened and what the damage was. Each department was double and triple checking their files, looking to see if anything had been stolen or altered. It was agreed that no one would bring up the details of the hack to anyone outside of the overseers' offices. There was no need to stir things up in the quadrants, and we didn't want anyone to know that someone was able to breach our security system.

Of course, even though we all kept our mouths shut, the Hacker announced their achievements all over every form of social media that was available to them. At first, we

269

tried to deny it through avoidance. Again, none of the overseers was allowed to discuss anything having to do with the hack to anyone outside of our offices. This worked for a very short amount of time, as people were starting to believe what the Hacker said. Stories from people who claimed that they had received their death dates were already adding to the issue. We no longer had a way of hiding what had happened, and we were forced to admit that we had been defeated.

Committees were formed to try to determine who the Hacker was, and a reward of $250,000 was offered to anyone who could provide us with the information that would catch them. While we waited for answers, we knew that we had to take action to prevent everyone from knowing what their death dates were. The microchipping system was designed so precisely, that if people started living their lives around their assigned dates, there were many possibilities for change that could negatively influence society.

It was agreed upon that measures would be taken immediately in an attempt to alter the existing death dates. If people found out their numbers, but we were then able to change them, it would render the work of the Hacker useless, and would signify a win for us. The group of scientists, computer programmers, and engineers that originally created the microchip system would meet once again to determine how we could change the information that was already in the system. Seeing how it mostly consisted around an algorithm, it seemed that the changing of the numbers in the database wouldn't be too hard. The issue was how to get the information changed within the actual microchips that were already implanted.

The group of brilliant minds couldn't come up with an infallible solution, but they were required to provide an answer. They had figured out a way to send a signal to each person's microchip that would override the previous date and implant the new one. It could be done wirelessly, so the person would have no idea that any changes were being made. During test runs, it only took a moment for the data to be fixed. They thought that if they sent out multiple signals from different computers at the same time, they could get every citizen's microchip modified within a single day.

Even though steps had been taken from the very beginning to fix what the Hacker did, it still took longer than anyone wanted to get the changes in place. It was over a month later when the signal was finally ready to be sent out to citizens in all four quadrants. Everyone stopped what they were doing to gather round and watch as the button was pushed that would start the transmissions. We all cheered as we watched the codes appear on the big screen. They were scrolling by quickly, denoting another person whose death date had been changed.

It took less than a minute before we heard the alarms going off. It was a sound that we were not familiar with, and various workers were bouncing around from screen to screen trying to figure out what was going on. Several minutes had passed before someone was able to find the source of the noise and turn it off. They were yelling something about stopping the signals, but no one understand what they meant. By the time their ramblings made sense, it was too late. More than 30,000 people had dropped dead suddenly, having had their chip accidentally activated during the reboot.

No one expected it to happen, and we were not prepared to deal with it. We still had hundreds of thousands of people left to change over, but we were forced to stop the process immediately. We all just kind of stood there, not knowing what to say or do next. This was way too many people to die in a day. The whole system was suddenly thrown out of whack. There was now a need to change everyone's dates to rebalance the population, but what if sending another signal killed more people?

It was a big mess, and would require a lot more manpower than the overseers had to clean it up. People would need to be hired and trained right away to help keep this situation under wraps. Would it even be possible to do? Alongside all of this, the Hacker still had not been found. As an overseer, my position was one of a leader who was supposed to train new hires in the ways of identifying, collecting, and cremating the bodies of citizens who had died. Normally, this was not a problem for me, as I had accepted the way of the microchip years ago. However, with this situation, I had a hard time reconciling what had happened. This was mass murder.

I asked if I could be reassigned, trying to find another position that didn't deal directly with the cleaning up of the mess that our group had created. I had to be careful and watch my words in my request. If any of the higher ups thought that I was shirking my duties, I would end up in a work camp, or possibly an even worse situation. At first, they didn't want to move me, as they needed to get many of the newly hired people trained quickly. I reasoned with them, explaining that most people were working on taking care of the current situation, and there were not a lot of people left to continue searching for the Hacker. As long as they were out there, they could continue releasing the death dates that they had, drawing more people in to go against the ways of the overseers. My argument was convincing enough to be reassigned, and I began my search to find the Hacker.

I struggle daily with the internal tug-of-war I experience with my job. The more I see what the results of the reboot did, the more I understand why the Hacker did what they did. I am good at my job, and I am sure that eventually I will find out who they are and can bring them in for justice. The question is, do I really want to?

ACKNOWLEDGMENTS

Many thanks are owed to the people who helped make this book possible. To all of those who read through my drafts and helped me hone my characters, I appreciate you. To the people behind their screens in NaNoWriMo, your smiling emojis and words of wisdom kept me going, even when I doubted myself.

Thank you to my parents, who have always encouraged and supported me in every endeavor I have tried. To my children, who kept telling me how proud of me they were. Finally, a very special thank you to my husband, who made sure I was given time to pursue this project. You took on extra responsibilities so that I could focus. I love you with all my heart and soul.

ABOUT THE AUTHOR

Ashe enjoys a chaotic life in the Southeastern United States. Originally from New York, she has made her home in the warmer climate. You can usually find her behind a laptop or a microphone.

She loves spending time with her family, including her two legged and four legged children. This is her first novel.

Made in the USA
Columbia, SC
13 February 2022